Reviews for *The Planet Dweller*

Jane Palmer's first novel Is a real find -definitely a specimen of higher lunacy. The Planet Dweller appropriates all the furniture of TV sci-fi and duly stands it on its head, with a wonderfully pragmatic absurdity - that's been done before, of course (Terry Pratchett, Douglas Adams), but not quite this way. How characters quite as insane as these - menopausal Diana and the radio-astronomer Eva, 11-year-old Julia, and the drunken Russian eccentric, Yuri - turn out to be as plausible as anyone you'd find in the average bus-queue, I do not know; but at one time or another I've met all these people. Real people are always more incredible than fiction likes to think...
Mary Gentle *Interzone*

A hilarious story in which the Earth is threatened by the deadliest life-form in the universe: the Mott. Diana, a menopausal mother, and Yuri, a practised drunk, are the two humans destined to fight them. They do have some help in the form of Dax and Reniola a pair of Torrons; uncomfortable in their new bodies they are eager if incompetent allies.
SFF Books

The 'familiar' voice - if their is one - should surely be credited to Jane Palmer, whose first novel 'The Planet Dweller' brings a much-needed note of sanity into the launch. Palmer has more in common with Muriel Spark than Marge Piercy. Her alien invasion of Earth takes place among the kind of people who cause havoc at the supermarket checkout. She also, with deft comedy, creates a Feminist who's literally the size of a planet, and that is a daunting prospect...
Jane Solanas *Time Out*

Jane Palmer's novel, The Planet Dweller quite
unashamedly a good sci-fi adventure, is really the odd
one out. It draws most on the traditional 'adventure'
strand of science fiction and quite cleverly weaves
together all the ingredients for a good read.

Liz Adams *Chartist*

The Planet Dweller is a much more traditionally sf
novel, and also funny in a Tom Sharpe/Douglas
Adams sort of way:

Paperback *Inferno*

Jane Palmer's first novel The Planet Dweller
comically (and Britishly) juxtaposes menopausal
female reality with a farcical chauvinist SF subplot
about the Molt and their plan to rule the galaxy. . .
The Planet Dweller is the most easily readable of the
four books, involving no noticeable shortforms.
Anything even slightly scientific is explained in a no-
lecturing manner, and if there is a feminist message, I
can't see it.

Guardian

The only first publication is also the only British one,
Jane Palmer's The Planet Dweller, and it is a world
away from the American novels. . . The Planet
Dweller has more in common with Dr Who than with
American theological feminism, including a sense of
humour.

David Sexton *Sunday Times*

Jane Palmer spins a confused but amusing tale of
earth menaced by extragalactic baddies. Her heroine,
Diana, a menopausal housewife and administrator of
an architectural museum, is original, sympatico and
fun.

Sunday Times Supplement

DUCKBILL SOUP

a sequel to

THE PLANET DWELLER & MOVING MOOSEVAN

by

Jane Palmer

DODO BOOKS

Other science fiction books by this author

BABEL'S BASEMENT
THE KYBION
THE PLANET DWELLER
MOVING MOOSEVAN
NIGHTINGALE
HUNDER
THE ATON BIRD

Fiction
BALD WENDY

CHAPTER 1

The duck-billed hadrosaur gazed at the red sun making a lurid dome on the horizon as it set. It looked like a nasty accident. The wistful sigh that escaped from the dinosaur's scaly beak was more like a child's being deprived of its favourite toy than that of a three-ton prehistoric herbivore. Bored with trying to digest cycad cones and dodge the bogs littered with the odd claw and snout of less fortunate animals, the hadrosaur delved into a fold of skin at her waist. Other members of the herd hadn't seen the need to evolve pockets and looked on in mild amazement as she pulled out a mobile phone.

They also didn't understand the language she used.

'Come on Dax, you've had plenty of time. I'm beginning to feel like a fool in this skin... What do you mean? My fault? You know more about atmospheres than I do. Why couldn't you have checked it out before we left..? Yes, of course I've got all the readings now. I'm waiting to come back. And make it snappy! Ever since I knocked out that tyrannosaur the rest of the herd have been giving me funny looks... Now those humans have got a brand new planet all to themselves you'd think they'd be happy. But no, they must have some water to keep the continents apart as well... Yes, I know their atmosphere is disappearing. It's just that they never seem satisfied...'

The herd of duck-billed hadrosaurs continued to graze with one eye on the look out for predators and the other on their sister with a mobile phone. Consequently they ate a good many things true vegetarians would have recoiled from and started to wonder if it wasn't time they tried to lose this member who, for some reason, was a conspicuous mauve. In a herd that was grey and orange, this played havoc with their evolving colour vision. They now wished they had a switch to turn it off.

The explanation for the talking hadrosaur was actually quite simple; it just required the imagination of a fantasy fanatic on LSD to grasp it.

CHAPTER 2

Diana, being a middle-aged single parent and, at first glance, quite domesticated didn't seem to be the sort of person who would have any sort of imagination.

Lifting her head from the pillow and wondering whether it was safe to wake up, she sighed with relief to see the sun rising in its usual place - as usual as could be expected that is, considering that the Earth was now orbiting on the opposite side of it. At least that grotesque piece of cosmic debris Reniola had found to replace the old moon had at long since set. Had there been any dogs, the sight of it would have cured them from wanting to howl. Its appearance had added a new cult worshipping extraterrestrial vampires to all the others devoted to Mother Nature, which regularly held ceremonies to try and reinstate the world rhythms human beings had ignored ever since they found out what caused babies.

Diana rolled over and asked herself yet again, 'Why did those stupid aliens go and have to put everyone on Titan?'

'You're talking to yourself again Mum,' sang out a voice from the bathroom.

Diana told her daughter, in a rather unmotherly way, to do something physically impossible with the shower head.

Julia was right, though. Diana was one of the only three human beings to know what had really happened, though the astronomer, Eva Hopkirk, had been taking one or two irrational and very accurate guesses. It would only be a matter of time before the knock at the door came and they would be obliged to explain how the Earth had shrank to under a third its size and the moon turned into a badly blasted asteroid, not to mention what had happened to all the animals conservationists had devoted their lives to preserving.

Orbiting on the other side of the sun, the Earth was now getting on very well with its new occupant, a planet dweller called Moosevan, and the animals, wild and domestic, were doing what came naturally to them without human interference.

Some astronomers had been concerned that Saturn was missing one moon. As Titan was the most speculated about phenomenon in the solar system, and last seen heading towards the Earth's orbit with unnatural speed, someone would soon put two and two together and come up with a headache.

Diana wearily washed and dressed while Julia saw herself off to school. All that frenetic dashing about in the morning just to make sure her daughter was pointing in the right direction with a packed lunch before nine o'clock no longer seemed to matter any more. A mysterious endowment that kept her bank balance topped up like some magical urn also meant that Diana had been able to give up her job at the architectural museum to spend most of the day watching the news, shopping for things she didn't really need and once again trying to talk her neighbour, Yuri, away from the gin bottle. He was one of the others who knew what had really happened to the Earth and found his old friend, booze, a better consolation than the sums of money placed in his building society account by aliens who wanted him to keep quiet about their existence. When the knock on his door came he wanted to be under the table and incapable of telling anyone his name and nationality.

It was about noon when Diana dawdled up the

meadow at the back of her terraced home to his ramshackle cottage. She couldn't get used to the idea that there was no longer any need to avoid treading on families of field voles or fresh cowpats. Even that diabolic horse once owned by Daphne Trotter, empress of the local gentry, had been spirited away to pastures where it was probably stampeding herds of peacefully grazing wildebeest or terrorising packs of baboons. Reniola not only lacked a sense of direction, her grasp of geography was nonexistent.

Had Diana known what miscalculations Reniola's companion, Dax, had made about the atmosphere of Titan, she wouldn't have been so resigned to the situation. The optimism of middle age insisted that the lack of oceans on this new world would bring people together; what it would do to the atmosphere hadn't crossed her mind. Many who had lived near volcanoes or in earthquake zones were just too grateful to have no more eruptions which demolished their homes or 50 foot waves slamming into their coasts to think about it either.

As a consequence, all the concerned ecologists monitoring the decline in the environment lost nerve and went underground to ponder on why there was no longer any Earth they could empathise with. They also risked persecution by churches recalling their medieval heydays and wanting to put the Earth, wherever it was, back at the centre of the Universe. Any others who had realised what was actually happening to their new ecosystem were more inclined to keep their heads under the bedclothes, including governments who daren't announce to rebellious populations that the atmosphere was growing less breathable. They already had their work cut out trying to cook up explanations for why their planet had shrunk to a third its original size.

Anarchy erupted in several countries, yet was

unable to supply butter any more than democracy could. It took some people, who thought that dairy products came ready packaged in plastic, a long while to comprehend that there were no longer any cows to produce the raw material.

Yuri's back door was open. The autumn air was warm and Diana didn't think it unusual. She sometimes wondered how Dax and Reniola had managed to copy the seasons so accurately but, as long as it wasn't permanent winter, it didn't bother her unduly.

There were voices inside the cottage. One of them belonged to Yuri. It sounded as though he hadn't managed to put away the amount of gin required to engage in rational conversation.

Diana silently stepped inside and peered past the parlour door curtain. Yuri was his usual dishevelled self; stained shirt, old jeans, and waistcoat half on. The small Russian astronomer's expression could veer between the blearily drunk to alertly angelic and, though there was no odour to suggest he didn't wash himself or his clothes, he seemed to wear a permanent tide mark like a halo. At one time he may have been a dapper shooting star of astrophysics. Now, almost burnt out, he was more like the grimy core of a comet composed of various mysterious substances. Those who knew him suspected that he played at being the shambolic eccentric to hide some knowledge they really wouldn't have wanted to learn about.

His visitor was a different kettle of fish. He had the air of an elegant pike about him. Diana didn't recognise the uniform, so assumed it belonged to the newly formed World Army. That was one of the few sensible ideas the UN had come up with since brotherly love went out of the window along with Glasnost and green awareness and they realised how easy it would be for so many countries to invade each other now there were no natural barriers to prevent it. Not only were most of the seas gone and mountain ranges flatter, the deserts had disappeared. So something had to be done to take people's minds off the fact they weren't after all, the most important individuals in the Universe.

The high-ranking UN officer, though well preserved, must have been nearing sixty. Diana hadn't any how he had arrived because there was no Land Rover or helicopter parked outside. She would have easily spotted a parachute, and the bus service from town usually didn't move until midday; something to do with saving fuel until the wind farms and solar parks were constructed. The soldier was also carrying a side arm. That would have been commented about on a No 9 bus, whose regular driver had no hesitation in confiscating catapults and stiletto umbrellas.

Diana stood as silently as she could just in case the man's trigger finger was as quick as his intelligent expression. She would have much rather gone to one of those bickering PTA meetings than engaged in meaningful conversation at that moment and, by the way Yuri slopped some tea into two enamel mugs, she could tell that he would have much rather been under the table.

The soldier gave a smile that shouldn't have been so engaging because of the thinness of his lips. His long, straight nose could have belonged to a lawyer and the expression in the sparkling eyes was boring away at Yuri's presence of mind.

'Come, come Sir.' The urbane tone seemed slightly patronising. 'I'm sure you can be a little more forthcoming than that. This is an international matter, you know. The situation affects everyone.'

Yuri took a noisy swig of tea and rinsed it round his mouth before swallowing it. Astutely, the officer unhooked a brandy flask from his belt and topped up the murky brew.

Yuri drank another deep draught and his scowl slackened a little. 'I tell you what I know, but about anyone else, nothing... You not believe me, though.'

'All human beings have been adapting to the impossible in their own ways, some very eccentrically, but I'm sure we are sensible people.'

'Do not humour me. My mother was black bear! I bite!'

Diana flinched. She had never seen Yuri bare his teeth at anyone before. By rights, those he still had should have been yellow, and she was surprised to see how sharp and white they were. Though the soldier paused for a moment, he wasn't deterred. His gentlemanly manner suggested he not only talked tigers out of trees, he went on to persuade them to become vegetarian.

The visitor pulled up a stool. 'Why don't we sit down?'

Yuri slumped heavily onto a chair by the table where he could look his adversary in the eye. The Russian should have been able to do that standing up because neither of them was over five foot six, but his elbows needed the support of the marble top so he could hold his head steady.

'What you think I know then?'

The soldier removed his cap to reveal a full head of immaculately groomed silver hair. The contrast between them was beginning to annoy Yuri.

'This must be in confidence of course. I will tell you the facts I have been furnished with in exchange for what you know.'

Yuri gave a blissfully sly smile. 'I tell you facts, but they not make sense. They put you in straitjacket before they believe you.'

'No one expected the explanation to be simple.'

'You think there are extraterrestrials, Colonel

Albright?'

The soldier caught his breath as though about to jump off a high wall. 'You mean, little green men?'

'No, big, ugly, toad like green men... but we come to him later.'

Colonel Albright hesitated. 'What sort of extraterrestrials then?'

'Shape-changing extraterrestrials.'

'You mean pure energy forms?'

'They are energy forms, but not that pure after what they do.'

'What did they do?'

'Us human beings out of our planet.'

The penny dropped with a pre-decimal clatter and the Colonel sat back to digest the revelation. 'We were evicted from the Earth by two energy forms?'

'They might have help-' something occurred to Yuri. 'You know where Earth is?'

'It took astrophysicists with hyperactive imaginations to make some bizarre calculations before they worked out that it was on the other side of the Sun.'

'Then you know what we sit on?'

'We assumed it to be Titan - admittedly with a rather dramatic face lift and manicure - but Titan all the same.'

Yuri shrugged. 'So, there you have it. We can do nothing. Just keep gun loaded and enjoy it.'

'Oh, how I wish we could.'

'I can do nothing... nor anyone else.'

'Well, old bean, I'm afraid that is going to be rather hard on the human race in that case.'

Yuri gave a suspicious squint. 'You mean what?'

'No oceans, no Great Ocean Conveyer Belt. You're an astronomer - elementary climatology. You work it out.'

This Yuri did in a nanosecond. The problem had

not occurred to him before because, beneath his burgeoning cynicism, a few molecules of his mind still believed the Universe had some benevolence left. The intergalactic intelligences that did this couldn't have really left everyone on a world without any way of renewing its atmosphere, even if their minds had been on other things.

The pike, having swallowed the minnow, gave a condescending smile. 'What were you going to tell me about this big, ugly, green man?'

Diana couldn't listen any more. She pushed the curtain aside and marched into the parlour. The Colonel looked up in mild surprise at the woman in the pink slacks. Despite her unbrushed hair and Garfield T-shirt, she was quite intimidating.

'All right, what's going on?' she demanded.

'Who are you?'

Yuri leapt up as though Diana were some delicate pet Pomeranian. 'My charlady. She know nothing.'

Diana exploded, which, on only a black coffee and Ryvita biscuit, was quite a feat for her at that time of day. 'Charlady! Bloody cheek!' She may not have been the world's best housekeeper, but there was no way she would have left anyone's room looking like the rough end of a pigsty.

The soldier rose and extended his hand. 'Good morning. My name is Colonel Albright. I take it you are one of the privileged few to know what is really going on?'

Diana snarled through her good teeth and hoped the plate of the others wouldn't slip out. She hated herself for liking the soldier. Until then she had regarded all men in military uniforms as being mindless, trained killers. This one sounded as though he would fall into a state of remorse for treading on a ladybird.

'Where do you want me to start?'

Albright withdrew a little, sensing that the question was more of a threat than offer of help. 'At the beginning?' he suggested.

Diana snatched Yuri's chair away and sat down before he could reclaim it. 'Right. It happened last midsummer's day.'

Albright nodded, as though realising she didn't expect him to believe a word of it and let her carry on. 'The early Earth accreted around a mechanism capable of activating a gravity corridor to another part of the Universe.'

'Put there by these interdimensional "intelligences",' added Yuri vehemently.

'Shut-up.' Diana returned her gleefully disconcerting gaze to the army. 'Also embedded in the Earth was the core that the new world would accrete around; a new home for a planet dweller.'

'Planet dweller..?' mouthed Albright.

'Called Moosevan. She once had her own world. Wore it like a shell.' His eyes widened, yet he said nothing. 'Had that device been activated by the two intergalactic agents sent to save Moosevan, the Earth would have been destroyed. They were persuaded to do something else instead.'

Albright's face might have lit up, even though he wasn't too sure their solution was anything to be elated about. 'So they let her inhabit the Earth?'

Diana nodded.

Albright gave a ragged sigh. At least that explained the problems they had with geography roaming about and what had happened to all the ICBM silos and their missiles, though it did save several countries the expense of decommissioning them. Pity the interfering aliens had transferred all the other weapons systems to Titan and left his old Labrador on Earth.

Albright fixed Diana with a penetrating gaze.

'Could you explain why the human race is now stranded on Titan and this Moosevan, with all the other animals, presumably inhabits the Earth?'

Diana shrugged. 'Moosevan's an easy going sort of creature... just couldn't cope with us.'

'I see. Why couldn't Moosevan have taken Titan instead and left us where we were?'

'Well, let's face it, the Earth was due for an MOT after what we did to it.'

It was true; even if the world's navies were furious at losing the oceans, massive areas of water on a planet the size of Titan would have meant humans rapidly having to evolve gills.

Albright shook his poll of immaculate silver hair. 'HQ won't like this at all, not at all.'

'Probably not, but they needn't blame us. We don't have any control over these characters any more than Kulp had.'

'Kulp?'

'You don't want to know about him.'

'Why not?'

'I'd prefer it to come as a surprise if your paths ever cross.'

Albright didn't like the tone of that. He replaced his cap. 'I don't suppose there's any way of contacting these intergalactic intelligences?'

'What? Dax and Reniola? Not that I know of. And I think we should know when we're well off. Look what they did the last two times they interfered.'

Albright seemed uncomfortable for some reason, yet said nothing.

Yuri withdrew his nose from the aroma of five star brandy in his mug. 'You mean we can do nothing to save atmosphere?'

Albright nodded. The most dramatic measures, even if the UN could get anyone to agree to them, wouldn't stop its deterioration. It took governments long enough to be persuaded that the ozone layer was disappearing and that cars cause pollution. If these entities hadn't switched planets, humans would have probably ended up with an atmosphere like Venus's. When humanity's paws couldn't be prized from the steering wheel of ecocatastrophe it's unlikely people would dash out onto the motorways to do rain dances and plant trees.

'What happens when volcanoes erupt?' Diana asked. 'The pollution would have nowhere to go.'

'There would not be enough rainfall to precipitate the fallout, so it's just as well this planet doesn't have any crustal movement,' explained Albright.

Yuri looked up sharply. 'You mean... there is no tectonic activity?'

The core of Titan may have moved once. It was now as inert as the population's capacity for self-control. Albright had never had to deal with hysterical crowds and would have sooner faced half a dozen marches of religious fanatics single-handed than calculated the prospect of them passing this world onto their descendants.

Diana thoughtfully poured herself a mug of Yuri's dingy tea. 'So what can you do about it?'

Albright gave a tight smile. 'Nothing I suppose, though I had to try. Your friend's address was passed on to me so it seemed pointless not to follow it up.'

'Who passed Yuri's address on to you?'

Albright was momentarily fazed. 'It wasn't his fault. Hardened agents would have found it difficult to resist those sorts of drugs - Not the sort of thing I'd go in for of course,' he added hastily.

Diana immediately knew he mean the English don who had reluctantly become entangled with them.

Salisbury was one of those people educated to a pitch of dangerous unworldliness, and had believed the worst that could happen to human evolution would be

the adoption of Webster's Dictionary by English
teachers. This was before he had an amorous planet
take a fancy to him, been chased by the army and a
large green alien, rescued by two shape-changing
entities, and then had to fend off a resentful Yuri who
was jealous because the planet dweller had been his
girlfriend.

'What you do to Salisbury?' Yuri blurted out as
though he was a bosom comrade instead of the thorn
that had punctured his few remaining illusions.

'I had nothing to do with this and am trying to
negotiate his release. I'm afraid the officer in charge of
that unit is as irrational as most other people at the
moment, though. Believes the man to be in league with
aliens from outer space.'

'Oh no, Kulp again. ' Diana sighed as though they
were talking about some annoying tomcat instead of a
galactic megacriminal.

'Perhaps if you managed to raise Dax and Reniola
they might rescue Salisbury?'

The suggestion was put so charmingly it was
difficult to believe it was blackmail.

'How?'

'If they are so intelligent, they might be able to
read thoughts.'

'If they had been reading mine over the past few
weeks it's very unlikely they'd want to come back.'

'Didn't you have some mental link with this
Moosevan as well?' Albright asked carefully.

'Yes, she talk to Moosevan,' Yuri accused Diana.

The Colonel's expression suggested that this was
what he really wanted to hear.

Diana gave a small laugh. Moosevan knew when
she was well off. Why should she try and help? The
planet dweller had no malice in her vast being, though,
so perhaps Diana should try. At worst, she would plug
into some transcendental group meditating on the

vibrations given off by new potatoes.

'Who else knows about Yuri?'

'Only me,' said Albright.

'Get Salisbury released and I'll help you.'

Albright gave a stiff nod. 'Very good.' He left silently without bothering to drop his calling card onto the much scuffed table in Yuri's hall.

Not waiting to see the skin congeal on her mug of tea, Diana followed him. By the time she stepped into the meadow Albright had gone, probably plucked up by some silent motorised balloon. She wandered back down to her terraced cottage and drew the curtains of her living room, where she relaxed in an armchair for some serious mind clearing. As all other problems now seemed such minor matters, she was surprised at how easily she managed it.

Calling up a planet orbiting on the other side of the sun should have been difficult, but now Moosevan had no romantic interests to distract her she should be more receptive to a sister spirit. The entity would have no doubt preferred to hear from Yuri or Salisbury. On the other hand - perhaps not. The planet dweller had gone off the Russian as soon as he had sobered up, and why hadn't she realised that Salisbury was in trouble? That was it! She was bound to answer as soon as she knew that the don was in danger. Without giving any thought to what Moosevan might do about it, Diana let her thoughts float free onto the orbit of the two worlds.

CHAPTER 3

When she woke, Diana knew that there was something she should have remembered. Instead of worrying about it, she made herself a coffee, boiled some rice, and opened the recipe book of government recommended dishes that could be made without any animal products. Ensuring that everyone had a balanced diet seemed to be their main priority now no one needed to negotiate over fish quotas and butter mountains, or worry about salmonella and BSE. The book listed ways to remove the bitter taste from acorns and make cheese with their pulp, 101 recipes for tofu which all had the consistency of latex, and tasted like it whatever you marinated it in, how to mould the putty cleverly created by removing the cellulose from straw and make cement burghers, and even how to bake flour with and without yeast - assuming you could get either from the secure storage vats governments were now hoarding them in since farmers were banned from using nitrates and had run out of manure. Only bakers and mice could get at the wheat, and the yeast was probably fermenting into a new life form that would take over as soon as human beings had been suffocated by the thinning atmosphere. Not to worry, it was wonderful what could be done with a carrot, a little sunflower oil, and bag of peanuts.

Diana suspiciously read the label on the jar of artificial yeast extract. This was now the wonder substitute for all meat flavours and supplemented the demand for Quorn. Chemists were working on more intestine numbing concoctions to improve on substitute meats but, not having any animals to test them on, found keeping within old government legislation heavy going.

Having tossed a few vegetables in hot oil to put with the rice, Diana had one of her inconvenient premonitions. They now came over her as frequently as hot flushes.

She walked to the front room to gaze out of the window.

There went Flora and Irene. They had always left at the same time to buy milk and cat food. Now they used that money to come back with a bottle of Spar wine and Danish pastry each. In their new home their pampered pussies were at that moment trying to work out how to catch a vole whilst avoiding the packs of pedigree hounds at liberty to do everything centuries of inbreeding had intended to anthropomorphise out of them. Strangely, Flora and Irene seemed much happier. Having discovered sherry and rum babas, they also started to wonder what else they had missed. There had never been any doubts when the vicar declared that animals didn't have souls but, as most of them had apparently gone to Heaven, the sisters felt free to natter about their growing atheism without being struck by lightning.

Then the real reason for Diana's premonition appeared. Eva Hopkirk's mud spattered car sped round the corner and screeched to halt outside the terrace of cottages. Eva was another lunatic of the local fold, though not one others tried to humour; a nod and quick departure was the safest way to greet the astronomer. There were always those who wanted to discuss their horoscopes, to which Dr Hopkirk would give an alternative reading and leave them thoroughly depressed, waiting for the tell tale signs of hepatitis B or watching pine cones that would predict an inundation overwhelming enough to make Noah give up. Eva had never been very kind to the gullible and had kept her marriage to Yuri more secret than the address of a tabloid reporter's bolthole.

'Damn,' swore Diana as a glimmer of what she should have remembered came back to her. The door bell rang and the thought fled.

Still wearing her ancient flapping overall, Eva strode into Diana's living room and dropped into the nearest armchair. She was a short, untidy woman who somehow took up enough space for a person three times her size.

'Now what?' Diana enquired without much enthusiasm as she poured her unlikely friend a glass of carbonated spring water.

'It's impossible of course...'

'What isn't?' Lately that seemed to be the only guarantee that it was actually happening.

Eva swigged back the water and hiccupped. 'I can't make it out.'

'You're talking astronomy, aren't you?'

'What else.'

'Why don't you pick on Yuri?'

'It's no use talking to him since he went back to the bottle. He'd never be able to see with his reflector what I'm picking up anyway.'

Diana smiled sarcastically. 'I always knew you'd be able to tune into some alien pop station with those radio telescopes one day.'

Eva ignored her. 'We've had a one and a half metre reflector installed.'

'What?'

'It's not calibrated yet, but when it is we'll be looking very closely at the solar system.'

'How are you going to pay for that?'

Eva gave a slow smile that could only mean one thing. 'I have a friend in high places.'

'She's a pigeon?'

'She has been monitoring the activity in an obscure part of the British Isles and sending the results to the UN.'

'So, she's a carrier pigeon.'

'And they are very interested in what's been going on in our little locality.'

Diana lifted the spring water bottle threateningly. 'What have you been telling the authorities about us?' The bottle began to fizz ominously.

Eva waved her aside like an annoying moth. 'The UN has recently appointed an astrophysics team. Given the way things were shifting about it seemed the most logical thing to do. I happen to be acquainted with one of the group leaders.'

'I still want to know what you've been telling her?'

'Oh, she's all right. Has to be with a name like Honey Paymaster.'

'Honey Paymaster?'

'Fijian. Used to collect exotic shells. Gone on to lead crystal now. You'd like her.'

'What have you told her?'

'Only that one or two planets and moons are starting to deviate from their orbits. Not enough observatories are still operating to confirm it and the amateurs have trouble phoning their findings in. It's difficult to tell anyway - us being on the other side of the sun - but Venus has certainly started to wobble, and Io is beginning to look a little wan.'

Deflated, Diana put down the bottle before it exploded. 'You know about us being on Titan?'

'Of course I do. Any prat capable of measuring a shadow can tell we're not on the Earth. Even if they didn't know the polar caps and oceans had disappeared, they must have noticed the unnaturally pronounced curve of the horizon.'

'Have long have you known?' demanded Diana.

'About you and Yuri galaxy trotting and hobnobbing with aliens?' Eva shrugged. 'The penny dropped when that observatory I was working in was suddenly pushed into the stratosphere by the mountain it sat on. I knew you had something to do with it. Couldn't make our what.'

'I see. At long last. Now you want me to tell you what's been going on?' Diana smiled maliciously. 'Well, I'm not going to.'

Eva viewed her with critical coolness. 'You shouldn't wear that colour lipstick. It doesn't match the bags under your eyes.'

'My last lipstick ran out a week ago, and anything manufactured with cow's blood or fish scales now costs a fortune.'

'Luckily I was never that keen on tripe or black pudding.'

'I'm still not saying anything. You laughed when Yuri tried to tell you about the asteroid belt reassembling itself ready to make a new world.' Diana marched into the kitchen. 'Are you stopping for rice and veg, or going?' she called over her shoulder.

'If I eat something can I stay?'

Diana tossed the meal together and tipped it onto two plates. She came back in and thrust one of them at Eva, giving her a spoon. 'Can't find any clean forks.'

Eva looked at the offering with a mathematician's eye as though trying to calculate the ratio of carrot to rice grain. 'You get more like Yuri every day.'

'You should go and see him every now and then.'

'Why?'

'You did marry him.'

'When I was younger had the occasional attack of compassion.'

'You told me you drew straws.'

'And no doubt you told Yuri.'

Diana glowered. 'You know I wouldn't be that mean.'

'He fancies you more, anyway.'

'All right. Let's talk about astronomy. I suppose you know that the atmosphere is going to pack up on us if we can't find some oceans from somewhere?'

Eva halted a spoonful of rice halfway to her mouth. 'Who told you that?'

Diana shrugged. 'Doesn't everyone know it?' she bluffed.

'Most people are still panicking because they can't buy a hamburger. God knows what they'd do if they found out they were going to suffocate as well.'

'Oh... somebody told me in confidence.'

'Who? Not that nutty English don who was driving

about the village, trying to remember where Yuri lives? Apparently had trouble reading his road map.'

Diana froze. 'What?'

'Harmless old soul. Saw him with Yuri not so long ago.'

Since very few roads were in the same place as they used to be a couple of months before, most people had a similar problem. It seemed odd that whatever shifted everyone to Titan needed to replicate the mayhem Moosevan had caused.

'How old?' demanded Diana.

'About our age.'

Diana shook her head. It couldn't be. Salisbury was supposed to be in the clutches of the army. Wasn't that why she had poked about in the hardly used recesses of her mind to try and raise Moosevan. The questions this revelation begged were too huge to contemplate at that moment.

'You haven't seen a UN officer, name of Colonel Albright, in these parts either, have you?' she asked as calmly as she could.

Eva looked surprised. Any uniforms wandering the locality would have soon been noticed. Daphne Trotter was the only person around there who wore boots since Bert Wheeler took to wearing trainers now there wasn't any wildlife to plunge through the undergrowth and shoot.

'Come on Mog, what's going on?' insisted Eva.

'Nothing. Only, if you do meet a man in a UN uniform, don't tell him anything.'

That's the last thing Eva would do; she hated uniforms and Honey Paymaster would have mentioned if the UN had sent someone else.

Diana managed to swallow her meal without choking. As soon as Eva left she pushed on her shoes and bounded up the meadow to Yuri's bungalow.

CHAPTER 4

The rest of the hadrosaur herd tried to sleep, but were
kept awake by the plod, plod, plod of tired footsteps
circling round them. The duckbill with the mobile
phone was making hard work of being a grazing
herbivore. As she had just routed a pack of sickle-
clawed deinonychids intent on having the herd's young
for a light snack, they were more inclined to tolerate
her eccentricities, despite insomnia. However, that
perpetual chattering into a small black box, deep sulks
when it didn't say anything that satisfied her, and
attempts to browse on all the wrong things was enough
to get on any dinosaur's nerves. And no herbivore
needed half a hundredweight of pebbles in its gizzard
to break down a dinner, even of cycad cones. This was
purely for chemical analysis of course though, like the
mobile phone, it would have been somewhat tricky to
explain that to them.

Their mauve sister also seemed to have a
disconcerting interest in the night sky. The herd had
never thought there was anything wrong with the two
massive moons until they noticed the strange twinkle
in her yellow eye, as though she wanted to alter that
arrangement.

The more the duckbill paced, the more she
wondered whether she was making the right decision.
Time was a funny thing and infinitesimal causation
could have cataclysmal effects. So, if the theory of
Chaos was stood on its head, it seemed reasonable to
assume that a major cosmic upheaval might only
trigger a minor imbalance in the order of things; and
this was no time to be faint-hearted about bending a
few Universal laws to manipulate wormholes in space-
time. In this backwater, who would notice anyway?

The mauve hadrosaur stopped pacing. Silhouetted
against the setting sun was a police box. A small

humanoid wearing a battered straw hat and carrying
an umbrella stepped from it, looked around, and then
stepped back inside again. The police box vanished.

'Strange,' the hadrosaur muttered to herself.
'Fancy carrying an umbrella in this climate.' Then she
started to pace once more.

CHAPTER 5

Salisbury had a gentle, forgiving nature, yet could not
make up his mind whether he preferred the
antagonistic, sober Yuri he had first known or the
amiably sozzled one. After Yuri made it known how the
army was supposed to have abducted him, the don
hoped the astronomer's story emanated from the gin
and they had not intended to do it. Whatever else had
happened when the human race had been transferred
to a new planet, Dax and Reniola had got everyone's
address right, and there was no way the army was
going to forget Salisbury's. He had never heard of
Colonel Albright, either. Although the soldier sounded
like a reasonable enough sort of fellow, Salisbury still
preferred to steer clear of anyone in a uniform.

For some reason, Yuri was anxious to get away
from his cottage, so Salisbury agreed to use half a
gallon of his precious petrol to head out onto the
twisting roads that mimicked the ones Moosevan had
created. When she had inhabited the Earth, the planet
dweller had visualised the English landscape as a knot
garden and designed vast fields of borage, rosebay
willow herb, and golden rod in elaborate carpet
patterns. Unfortunately, instead of using gravel paths
to outline her creations, she chose tarmac.
Consequently, most motorists unlucky enough to
encounter one of these roads burnt up all the fuel in
their tanks before they could find their way out. It
didn't help that, having transferred the road network

to Titan exactly as Moosevan had left it on Earth, Dax
and Reniola hadn't included any offshore oil reserves.
As a consequence, the massive knot gardens became
dotted with abandoned cars. Fortunately Salisbury
anticipated the problem and wasn't caught out that
easily, despite his problem reading a conventional road
map.

'Look,' Salisbury eventually said after just
managing to avoid a strategically placed lily pond.
'Why is it necessary to drive out this far? We're going
to get lost if we carry on.'

Yuri looked furtively about the deserted
countryside. 'Okay, we stop here.'

Salisbury stopped his green and mauve car into a
lay-by and they got out.

The countryside without bird song was unnerving
and the silence made Yuri shudder, even after several
stiff drinks. 'I do not think anyone listen,' he
announced unsurely.

'Why should they for goodness sake? The army I
encountered wouldn't have had the wit to track down a
herd of elephants in the same barn.'

'It is not army you met which I think about.'

'Oh,' Salisbury recalled. 'Albright. UN, you say?
Not likely to be engaged in any sort of mischief, I
would have thought. They've got a reputation to live up
to now. Too many countries with vulnerable borders
depend on them.'

'There is something sinister about this Albright. If
you did not give him my address, then who..?'

'Goodness knows. I was the only one the military
seemed keen on beating up.'

'They think you were in league with Kulp.'

'How could they have thought I'd team up with
someone as unscrupulous as that green slug?'

'As you say - they are not very bright.'

Salisbury sat down on a fallen tree trunk and

studied the great slabs of bracket fungi growing from
it, wondering whether they would fit into a frying pan.
'Do you realise how many nights' sleep I've lost since
meeting you and your green friends?'

'Very, very many I should think,' Yuri admitted.
He knew the problem well. 'You should become
alcoholic like me.'

'The thought of some planet creature having a
crush on me nearly did drive me to the port.'

'Ah, Moosevan. She has no one to flirt with now.'
He noticed Salisbury's expression become strangely
frozen. 'What is matter?'

'I'm not sure. I don't like to think about it.'

'Why not?'

Salisbury took a deep breath. 'I thought you might
help.'

'How?'

'She fancied you long before she met me.'

'So?'

'When I sleep, I hear this voice - No, that's not
right. These thoughts somehow arrive in my mind.'

'This I understand.'

'It's eerie.'

That was Moosevan's way of communicating. If she
did have a mouth and was capable of speech, everyone
on that side of the solar system would have heard her
romantic overtures.

'What she say?' Yuri asked slyly.

'I think she is trying to tell me something.' The don
scratched his nose. 'I'm not sure what. I wake up in a
cold sweat before she gets round to it.'

Yuri threw out his arms. 'Ah, she wants you to join
her.'

'That's probably why I wake up before I can find
out.'

'Why you not listen?'

'I am not travelling, by any means, to the other

side of the sun to exist on a planet that is swarming with vengeful wildlife, and which is home for an erotic entity who could live for half of eternity.'

'You must humour her.'

'I wish you would take this seriously. Why should I humour her for goodness sake?'

Yuri was suddenly pensive. He stood and thought for a few moments. 'This is good question. Now she has Earth, there is nothing we can offer.'

Salisbury knew he had wasted a journey and only hoped he could find the way back to his college before being missed. He stood up. 'I don't suppose you would have any objection to me seeing Diana before I leave?'

Yuri shrugged. 'Diana would not forgive me if I spoke for her.'

On the way back to Yuri's bungalow both men were silent. New nightmares were pushing their way up through the creaking floorboards of their sanity.

When they arrived, Diana was sitting in Yuri's parlour sipping gin. Salisbury coyly embraced her as though she was some fearsome aunt back from the dead. Diana was just relieved to find him unmarked and his nervous, highly strung self, which he was quite entitled to be. Not everyone gets pursued by the army, a passionate planet, and evil green aliens in the same day. To distract them from going over the events that had led up to the human race being banished to one of Saturn's moons, she brewed a pot of tea in the hope that would prove less corrosive than Yuri's cheap gin.

'I've something to tell you, Salisbury.' Diana suspected the don had a Christian name, which he hadn't mentioned for fear of blushing every time she used it. 'I didn't start to remember until Eva came round...' she stopped awkwardly.

Salisbury knew that it had to be something pretty absurd to make Diana hesitate. 'You've been hearing from Moosevan as well.'

'Albright wanted me to contact her.'

'He told you I was being interrogated by the army?'

'Promised to get you released if I co-operated.'

Salisbury took a mug of tea from Diana and sat on the sofa's only intact cushion. 'I don't like it; I don't like it at all. Perhaps the army unit after me supplied him with false information for some reason.'

'What reason?' asked Yuri.

'To help confuse the UN perhaps.'

'Why? They are already more confused than moths at midday anyway.'

Diana looked absently at the cracked teapot. 'I don't think I really want to know the answer to any of this.'

The wail of a distant siren scorched the ensuing silence as a police car in distress tried to find its way out of one of Moosevan's mazes.

'My large lilac tree has changed colour,' Salisbury suddenly announced. 'It had white blooms in the spring then, in the middle of the summer, burst into bright mauve flowers. Very odd.'

'You know what I think,' Diana mused sternly.

'What?' Yuri muttered non-committally.

'I think we're being set up.'

'What? Again?'

'If anyone on this planet is going to be set up, it would have to be us.' Diana put down her mug. 'I have to go. Julia will want something for tea.'

'Can she not peel her own turnips?'

'The child hasn't quite been reduced to that sort of diet.'

'I find that mixing nuts with bulgur wheat and rice quite palatable,' suggested Salisbury.

'You hungry then?'

'Not really. My appetite declined at the thought of never being able to tackle a piece of red Leicester again.'

Diana glowered at Yuri. 'Don't you dare say that it serves all of us right.'

Yuri smiled smugly. That very sentiment permeated his misanthropic soul with no regrets at the human race being deprived of their staple diet. He preferred animals to people and even might have managed a friendly exchange with Daphne Trotter's horse given time, despite it kicking his garden gate off its hinges.

'Well,' sighed Salisbury. 'I suppose we can only wait and see what happens.'

Diana gave him a puzzled look. 'You aren't going back home, are you?'

'Why not?'

'Albright was not some illusion thought up by Yuri and me.'

'Do you really think they would arrest me then?'

'Don't you?'

Salisbury considered this. They would.

'You stop here,' Yuri ordered, afraid Diana might offer to put him up instead.

There was no choice. However much Salisbury would have preferred to stay with Diana, propriety would not allow it, and even Yuri's cottage was preferable to some barrack cell.

That night Salisbury made his bed on the lumpy sofa not long enough to accommodate his height, with a blanket that must have been woven with teasels and in a cutting draught the heavy velvet curtain over the door was too short to stop. It was like being in his old college dormitory; he even had one of the attendant nightmares to remind him of its horrors. By the time morning arrived and he had gently worked the crick from his neck, he wondered why he had ever built up such an aversion to Moosevan invading his dreams.

CHAPTER 6

Kulp was one of the few green Olmuke left. Most of the others had been turned bright pink by the dye with which he had sprayed their planet in a fit of resentment. As he was now imprisoned there for misdemeanours great enough to make him criminal of the millennium, his colour would have been somewhat conspicuous even if he had managed to escape.

His two partners in many crimes, Tolt and Jannu, had long since taken off to make their own fortunes with an uncharacteristic determination to abide by the law. Kulp assumed Dax and Reniola had scrambled the molecules of their brains when they transmitted them back through the gravity corridor to the Olmuke home world.

There was no justice; the three Olmukes' escapades on the Earth's were nothing compared to the interference of Dax and Reniola.

The decaying galaxy Kulp came from had been dominated and picked clean of its natural resources by the Mott. These warlords had evolved from a competitive species that eventually ran past itself, only to be liquidated by its own androids.

While the Mott females remained tuskless, two-legged and three eyed, the males had genetically engineered for themselves four legs (each), protruding teeth so long they couldn't chew the meat they were so adept at killing, and one eye. No designer of a video game could have thought up aliens that sometimes didn't believe their own reflections when inadvertently glimpsing them. Their appearance had been intended to terrify the rest of the galaxy, and anyone laughing instead had been instantly exterminated, along with any others suspected of having a sense of humour.

The only beneficial thing about the haphazardly genetic transformation of the male Mott had been that

they found it impossible to mate, so the Mott females
were obliged to rely on artificial insemination, much to
their relief. When all the males were slaughtered by an
army of their own androids because they had forgotten
how to switch them off, the female Mott decided to go
back to the blueprint for the species and engineer a
male who didn't look like a badly made clothes horse
sprouting lavatory brushes. Tolt and Jannu had been
happy to sell their services to that cause, leaving Kulp
to steam and plot in his cramped cage, where he
reluctantly concluded that there was nothing else for
it. Pink it would have to be. All he needed to do now
was remember the formula for the dye and get a
Dringle to unlock the door.

Anyone else with Kulp's sharp memory would
never have been able to live with their conscience, but
several coatings of compulsive greed insulated this
Olmuke's misgivings. Having had time to confront the
wickedness of his deeds, Kulp came to the conclusion
that they had been a pretty good idea after all. It
would be even better if he came up with something to
improve on them. Reordering the Galaxy to suit the
needs of the nouveau riche who had arisen since the
male Mott had been exterminated wouldn't be that
much of the crime anyway.

As the Mott females had managed to hang onto
some of the Mott wealth, with the co-operation of a few
pragmatic androids, they were in a position to govern
what was left of the old empire. Political alliances
didn't appeal to them, though; some of the Motts' allies
were almost as repellent as their unlamented mates.
The females had open, charitable natures the complete
opposite of their husbands, were far from glamorous or
terrifying, and their frocks were always the wrong
colour. Their inferiority complex enabled the younger,
upwardly mobile and downwardly altruistic Mott
collaborators to grab power with however many

appendages they had. Races that had been cringing under the hooves, or up the backsides, of the Mott suddenly blossomed into currency butterflies. As soon as planets were once again able to manufacture enough to survive, their industries were bought up by a new galactic counsel. They were resold, share by share, to entrepreneurs who thought that the gold plating on their diplomatic satchels came from the eggshells of an extinct asteroid dragon, and that those who wanted to grow food instead of live off burghers made from industrial waste, were anarchists.

This new order may have been a tyranny but after the Mott, who had done most of their diplomacy with blasters, it at least looked smarter, flitting about in personalised space buggies from one asteroid party to another.

Kulp had no time for them. To him, greed was something to be savoured during the long steamy evenings. Unfortunately only these nouveau riche had enough wealth to afford what he planned to sell and this yuppie empire needed new, extremely expensive playthings it could show off.

Asteroids were great places to have parties for as long as they could hold an atmosphere, only to disintegrate when all those personalised space buggies blasted off after they were over. Planets - the ecologically sound type with enough atmospheric molecules to hold a tune - were really where it was at. If the planet dwellers hadn't got in there first, there would have been plenty to go round. After what had happened to Moosevan's original planet - it had ended up as a cosmic cinder after Kulp had tried to evict her from it - Kulp should have known better. This time he was convinced he had the perfect solution; no need for space distort nets or clumsy robots to carry explosives. The creature who could do it, probably not free of charge - that was something he would have to negotiate - existed. All those worlds now monopolised by other planet dwellers could then be sold as the ultimate holiday homes to entrepreneurs whose most bankable commodities did not include scruples.

Kulp was still in his cage, though. Whenever one of the guard Dringles brought him a meal, he offered them snippets of what could be accomplished if he were only let loose on a galaxy that, through experience, had learnt to be very suspicious, but not how to duck. At first they thought he was inventing everything; the Olmuke were not renowned for their flights of fancy. Then one of them had enough imagination to read the list of charges against the prisoner. It was pretty impressive.

Dringles were uncomplicated creatures. They waddled like amiable teddy bears, yet could pick out every insect in a swarm without once getting stung: this they did frequently because they were fond of honey; not the sort of sweet stuff humans like. Its narcotic effect could last weeks and increase their IQ tenfold. It must have been in short supply at that moment because one or two started to listen to Kulp. The Dringles resented being used for the tasks the Olmuke found it too tedious to bother with, but had never been able to work out what to do about it. Perhaps Kulp was the solution.

It had to look like an innocent break-out of course, so the Dringles found the chemicals required to turn him pink and bribed the attendant of one of the aristocracy's space ships to turn its back at the right moment.

Once transformed into glowing pink and fitted with a space uniform, Kulp fed in the code that unlocked his prison door, and then darted through the metropolis to the spaceport. The only problem he encountered after boarding the silver ship was a large, hairy Dringle sitting at its controls. Bright they may not have been, but no creature aware of Kulp's record would have trusted him out of their sight. There was nothing Kulp could do about it. The Dringle was quicker on the draw, and that amiable pussycat smile was more deceptive than a hungry polar bear's. He just hoped the creature would lose its enthusiasm when it knew where they were going.

It didn't help sweeten Kulp's temper to discover that the Dringle could speak fluent Olmuke. Most of them just grunted and waved their arms a lot, which hardly mattered because nobody ever paid attention to them anyway.

'I hope you don't think I'm going to let you drive this ship?' Kulp counted on the Dringle understanding the daggers in his tone.

'One of us had better drive it.' The Dringle smiled. 'The theft alarms have just gone off.'

'Oh shit,' Kulp cursed. 'Why didn't I think more of Tolt and Jannu?' With reflexes like a striking snake's, Kulp turned on the ship's power and made it vault upwards before its computer had time to digest what was happening.

CHAPTER 7

'Well, what did he say?' asked Eva as she gloated over the observatory's new reflector.

Honey Paymaster gave a bemused grin. 'Colonel Albright has no idea who this visitor is. He was going to be sent here from the UN, but wasn't due to arrive for another 36 hours.'

'Who the hell then ..?'

'Colonel Albright is more interested in knowing how this impostor found out about his movements. That was classified information.'

Eva shrugged. 'Well, it's hardly the surprising given the people Diana and Yuri keep bumping into.'

'Why?'

'You wouldn't believe me if I told you the half of it.'

'You weren't the only one hijacked by the geography when this planet started to have a fit. I was on Lake Erie when it disappeared! Had to walk five miles to find out where I was.'

'What were you doing in the middle of Lake Erie?'

Honey pulled some papers from her briefcase. 'Why not stop playing with that telescope for a moment and sign these papers.'

'With blood, or just the usual biro?'

'These are for the telescope's housing. You've already sold your soul for the reflector.'

Eva pulled out a stub of pencil from an overall pocket and scoured her signature in the places indicated. 'I haven't spotted anything else yet. The only mathematician who could calculate a solution from the figures we have hit the gin bottle a couple of weeks ago.'

'Well, after being married to you...'

'How did you know?'

'I was one of those to draw a long straw, remember?'

'Oh, yes - some while ago, that.'

'How is Yuri?'

'I still don't understand him. Though I'm now sure he isn't so mad. With his mind he could untie the Gordian knot, but ask him to find the eyepiece of his reflector after a few gins - It might make him a little happier if I were to let him loose on this telescope, I suppose.'

'Think he would find out anything?'

'If it wasn't there, he could always conjure something up.'

CHAPTER 8

Diana replaced the binoculars in her shopping bag. Julia had only grudgingly lent them and her mother wouldn't have heard the last of it if she had left them in the long grass.

She got up to stalk her quarry and soon wished she had put on a pair of flat shoes.

As before, the vehicle Albright had arrived in was nowhere to be seen and, by his nonchalant stroll, he had hardly walked all the way from London.

To Diana's annoyance, her furtive vigil in the tall grass by Yuri's cottage had been a waste of time. Colonel Albright was making his way to the back door of her terrace instead. Now she was going to look a fool bounding down to meet him.

Why did the man have to be so likeable? All the upright, honest, and totally trustworthy men she had met before then had been either crashing bores or totally eccentric; this one was probably married to another colonel and spawned a regiment before his fortieth birthday.

Taking off her shoes to ruin yet another pair of Julia's tights, Diana managed to make it half way down the meadow. As he turned to see her, she pulled up abruptly to casually saunter the rest of the way, shoes still in hand.

'Yuri isn't in, you know,' she called out, and resisted adding that he was travelling the countryside with the prisoner Albright had promised to rescue.

'Yes, I know.' Albright immediately realised that he shouldn't have admitted it.

Trying not to look too breathless, Diana joined him. 'Go inside. You'll only find Julia watching some soap.'

'Soap?'

'Yes. Now there aren't any budgies, she has to

watch something.'

The Colonel detected the sound of distant battle in her tones and wondered if he wasn't going to find an ambush instead.

'Caught you,' Diana muttered under her breath as she slammed the plug into the kettle and switched it on. Revolver or not, she secretly turned the key in the back door and pocketed it. 'Do you take sugar?'

'Only in coffee.'

'Good. It's tea and I haven't any left. Julia!'

Albright flinched and wondered how deaf her offspring could be.

'Yes Mum?' came a high pitched voice from the front room.

'Orange juice!'

'Five minutes.'

'Now!'

'Oh Mum - Aunt Bernie's dog's just fallen down a mine shaft and is about to die and the vet can't do anything about it...'

'Of course she can't, you silly child. They've got to write all the animals out of the script, haven't they.'

'Oh Mum...'

'It's not my fault! '

Defeated, Julia stomped in as the credits began to roll.

Diana slopped orange juice into a tumbler and tossed some ginger nuts onto a plate. 'Don't ask me what happened to the milk again. You would never drink it when we had any.'

Julia's gaze was on Albright. 'Wasn't going to.'

'You may return to the bright box of many wondrous colours.'

'Oh Mum...'

'This is a personal conversation. Go.'

'Oh Mum...' Julia took her orange juice and biscuits and returned to the front room.

Diana ushered her visitor into the living room and indicated an armchair. As Albright sat down, she pulled up another chair to face him. 'I suppose you want to know how I got on?'

'Yes, that is why I called.' He cautiously took a sip of tea.

'I did manage to get through to Moosevan.'

Albright's face lit up with a little too much enthusiasm. 'Wonderful.'

'It might have been some interference in the ether, but she seemed puzzled,' Diana lied.

'Puzzled?'

'Puzzled that you would want to try and contact Dax and Reniola.'

'Really?'

'Biscuit?'

'No, thank you.'

'Real soya flour.'

'No, really. Please go on.'

'Yes. Apparently Reniola has managed to transport herself back to somewhere in the distant past and Dax...'

'Yes?' he bluffed.

'Moosevan can't think of any reason why Dax would want to speak to her. She certainly doesn't want to speak to Dax.'

The soldier's expression changed as though the strings holding up his amiable smile had suddenly been cut. 'But they gave her a whole fertile planet and viable biosphere. What's the matter with-' Albright cut his words short.

Diana smiled. He was trapped. 'Yes, they did, didn't they. Pity it was ours.'

Albright was not a man to bluster, yet a glimmer of panic crept into his eyes. 'Yes, but-' on the verge of admission, the front door bell rang.

'Damn!' swore Diana.

'I'll get it Mum,' sang out Julia.

'If that's Eva...' Diana listened for the astronomer's gravelly voice. Instead, her ears thrummed in amazement as they heard the familiar tones.

Julia was silent for longer than was natural for a spirit born to chatter. 'Mum ..?'

'Who is it?'

Her daughter paused for so long Diana wondered if she had forgotten what her vocal cords were for.

'You'd better go through,' Julia eventually said.

Diana turned to see the intruder.

Albright rose... to find himself facing the real Colonel Albright.

CHAPTER 9

Even if the Dringle did know how to fly the stolen space ship, its nails were far too long and kept snagging on switches with near disastrous consequences. Kulp managed to make the hairy lump understand that he was the better pilot and persuaded it to watch the gyroscope scanner. This served no useful purpose other than keeping its pleasure centres entertained with enough kaleidoscopic patterns in perpetual movement to hypnotise a large flock of chickens.

At last Kulp was able to program a course to Planet Lightning. It was seldom referred to by its catalogue number because those suddenly confronted by the world didn't have time to look it up. This planet's density had increased to the point where it had swallowed its many moons and a thin spiral of material from the solar system's mild yellow sun was being drawn into its maws. By rights, only another star should have possessed these properties, so the entity made no astronomical sense. Why Kulp believed he was immune from its appetite was only something known to the depths of his egotistical mind.

When the Dringle realised where Kulp was taking them, it considered getting off at the nearest mining station and applying for work as a radioactive dust extractor attendant. Its ego only needed the smaller fruits of corruption. Didn't Kulp know that the lightning entity could leave its planet to pursue prey for light years if it liked the taste? Didn't the Olmuke know that it could dodge dimensions and lay in wait in gravitational blips spun from its own being? Didn't Kulp know that what he was doing was very, very dangerous? Evidently he did. The Dringle couldn't comprehend what drove one of the Galaxy's greatest criminal minds or how Kulp had managed to resume his natural green complexion. The Dringle wasn't sure whether it was grateful for this or not. It certainly made him look even less digestible. But then, they were such small fry the lightning entity was unlikely to be interested. Unfortunately Kulp had discovered the frequency that would announce their presence by the time they reached Planet Lightning.

The irregular world, which looked as though it had been studded with shattered glass, revolved massively before them.

The lightning entity answered Kulp's a signal by sending out a pulse of energy that made their ship shudder. Kulp and the Dringle felt themselves slowly being drawn towards its mighty, crushing maws.

CHAPTER 10

After once more checking that the haystack was still concealing his car from the country lane, Salisbury lounged back in the autumn sunshine and tried to concentrate on Coriolanus. The words of the pompous Roman turncoat kept evading him and he realised he should have selected a play for his students that contained a character he could have had some sympathy with. They probably thought he had more in common with Sir Andrew Aguecheek or some rude mechanical. Though one of the college's most respected tutors, Salisbury's self doubt still ruled his life. In his childhood, when being cast for Christmas pantomimes, he had never been allowed to portray anyone with more machismo than Snow White, and only then because he was too tall for a dwarf. The English don pushed away the intrusive horrors of adolescence and tried to convince himself that anyone reaching their late fifties had the right to believe themselves an adult.

Yuri had escaped such unsettling recollections. Youth had never bothered him. His troubles began when he grew up and could no longer plead innocence. His thoughts were now turning over calculations he made the night before when his ten-inch reflector had detected the occasional misalignment here and slight wobble there. As they were too dramatic for any sensible phenomena, he knew it had to be something to do with Dax and Reniola. Exactly what they were up to was beyond even his imagination. He could only hope they had returned to patch up the damage done during their previous visit. They surely had to be answerable to some almighty entity even if it was so evolved it lived in several dimensions at the same time, and thought the Earth little more than a molecule with an annoying perturbation.

But that was unjustified optimism. Yuri thought it more likely that Dax and Reniola were collecting together other bodies in the Solar System to increase the size of Titan. As he was living on it at that point in time, the consequences didn't bear thinking about. On the other hand, they might have been cobbling together a completely new planet, one that would have a few extras, like oceans and crustal movement; a

place where the horizon didn't fall away so steeply it
gave susceptible people vertigo, something large
enough to hold onto a breathable atmosphere by the
time Titan's disappeared.

Salisbury noticed Yuri deep in thought and it
worried him.

'Think we should get back to Diana now?' he
suggested as though she were a priceless porcelain left
in the care of a car crusher.

'Why this worry about Diana?' snapped Yuri. 'You
are always on about Diana as though she has brain of
marshmallow.'

'I'm concerned about her. She shouldn't be involved
in a dangerous situation like this.'

'Last time, she save us from dangerous situation
like this.'

'That's not the point.'

Yuri pulled out a whisky flask, muttered
something in his mother tongue, and then took a
swallow of the firewater. He coughed violently as some
of it found its way into his windpipe.

'Why don't you try watering down that poison with
gin?' Salisbury suggested unhelpfully.

Yuri preferred to choke than admit he was also
worried about being away from Diana for so long. He
pulled himself up from the hay and buttoned his
waistcoat. 'How long it take to get back?'

'About an hour. You would insist we kept well
away from anything resembling a straight road.'

'The less we are there, the less chance they find
us.'

'You are quite paranoid.'

'You would invite Baba Yaga and Vodyanoi on
picnic.'

'Friends of yours?'

'And offer them cucumber sandwiches.'

Salisbury gave up and climbed into the car. Yuri

joined him and they wended their way back to his cottage in silence.

CHAPTER 11

Kulp dashed about the control of the stolen spaceship, operating its reverse thrust with one hand whilst trying to reconnect to the lightning entity's illusive frequency with another. For all its sophistication, the ship's communication system refused to tune into the wavelength. He kicked the console several times, denting its reinforced housing and the Dringle wondered whether it had been such a bright idea to threaten the Olmuke after all. This was one demented mega mind blowing its top like a peppermint tornado with a perspiration problem.

Faster and faster Kulp and the Dringle fell towards Planet Lightning and the cosmic entity's stomach, which was growling like a fusion furnace.

Kulp armed the ship's self-destruct system, just in case. If the entity had any sense at all it would detect it counting down. The lightning creature had more sense than Kulp credited it with and, as soon as they were close enough, realised that Kulp and the Dringle were far from tasty morsels.

Their craft juddered to an abrupt halt and it hung in the turbulent atmosphere like a stunned moth.

Having lost control of the ship, Kulp tried not to panic and the Dringle blew out the strands of hair it had swallowed in fright to watch a pattern like an explosion of multi-faceted icebergs forming on the monitor.

'Olmuke,' throbbed a voice so low, it must have loosened welds in the craft's hull. 'What do you want here?'

'I...' Kulp started, and then pulled himself together. 'I was trying to contact you.'

'Why?'

There was something wrong, here. A creature so different from an Olmuke might have at least made some attempt at an accent and not sounded like the regional tyrant who had threatened to use his intestines to make fireworks to celebrate the defeat of the Mott. Then he realised that the infernal entity was plugged into his mind. Despite what it found there, it decided to carry on the conversation.

'You understand me?' Kulp uttered foolishly.

'Obviously.'

'No one has ever contacted you before?'

'No one has ever been stupid enough to get this close.'

Kulp was becoming unsure about his risky adventure. The fact that the entity also appeared to have manners was even more disconcerting.

'What is your name?' it roared.

The Olmuke gulped. 'Kulp. '

'And your companion?'

'He's just a Dringle.'

'My name is Krykal.'

The fact that an entity that all-consuming needed a name threw Kulp for a moment. Perhaps it actually had parents and did not evolve from an anomaly spewed out by cosmic turbulence after all. Discovering that he did not know so much as he had always believed made Kulp hesitate for a moment. What had he let himself in for?

'What do you want?' demanded Krykal in a voice still resonating as though it was at the bottom of a gravitational whirlpool.

'I have a proposition to make,' Kulp announced as firmly as he dare under the circumstances.

'What proposition?'

'I understand you are able to leave your planet?'

'Why do you need to know?'

'Because I know it is impossible for planet dwellers to survive outside theirs for very long.'

'Planet dwellers!' roared Krykal. 'I eat planet dwellers!'

'Now that was what I had come to see you about.'

'They are only small snacks, not worth the distance I would have to travel to reach them.'

'What about entities with more energy than a billion planet dwellers?'

Krykal paused. It knew what Kulp was driving at. Before the fall of the Mott, the antics of two certain entities had been the talk of the galaxy, and on frequencies Krykal could detect. 'You mean those creatures called Dax and Reniola?'

'Yes. How about them?'

'I could live off their substance for aeons.'

'I know where they are.'

'Where?' the voice reverberated in his head.

'Before I tell you, how about devouring one or two tasty planet dwellers for starters?'

'Why?'

'I need their planets - preferably intact.'

The voice fell silent for some while. Then the ultimate question all things mortal and immortal doing a deal with Kulp ask, 'How can I trust you?'

'The Dringle here trusts me.'

As the Dringle was still shivering, it could have been nodding and the creature's brain was so stunned Krykal was unable to detect whether it could even remember its own name.

Kulp went on. 'I also have a gravity corridor that can take you straight to Dax and Reniola.'

'You will come with me.'

The last thing the Olmuke intended to do was go back to meet the very entities who had crushed his self esteem and dispersed his molecules so many times his ego fainted whenever he thought of them. Yet he

needed to be rid of the couple once and for all. He had
no choice but to agree. 'All right.'

'Before I devour the planet dwellers.'

'Now look-'

Something slammed into the ship and sent its
occupants spinning. It was a perverse relief to discover
that Krykal wasn't so courteous after all and helped
Kulp to get a better measure of the creature - albeit
with a pretty long ruler. 'All right! All right! I'll do it.'
So what did it matter if the lightning entity devoured
Dax and Reniola sooner or later. At least they would
finally be out of the way.

It was at this point the Dringle decided it wanted
to be paid off and taken to the nearest habitable planet
while some still existed. Somehow the words wouldn't
come and Kulp was already plotting a course to the
portal of the stand-by gravity corridor through which
he could reach Earth. His original one had been on a
planet with an atmosphere and inevitably life forms
were attracted to it. Before the intelligent fungi that
was catapulted through it could dismantle the portal,
the gravity corridor became unstable, and snapped
shut like a piece of cosmic elastic and ended up as a
singularity at the centre of a rather surprised neutron
star.

CHAPTER 12

Colonel Albright gazed at his double for a few moments
before announcing, 'I don't know what's going on here,
but I certainly intend to find out.'

'You won't believe it,' Diana advised.

'I didn't believe Honey Paymaster when she told
me I had a doppelganger, but then, that's not the only
unlikely thing I've refused to believe just lately.'

'You must be building up quite a log jam.'

'I find that accounting for the smaller absurdities

first helps free up space for the major implausibilities
without doing severe damage to one's sanity.' Albright
gave the impostor a steely glare. 'I think this
implausibility should be ferried to a saw mill as soon
as possible.'

'What's a doppelganger?' asked Julia.

'There is a quite simple explanation for this little
deception,' said Albright's double. 'Unfortunately, I
can't allow you to tell anyone else about it.'

'Can't you indeed.' Albright drew his revolver.

Diana sighed. 'Oh put that thing away. Apart from
being useless, I don't want holes in the furniture.'

Colonel Albright wasn't to be dismissed that easily.
'Excuse me, Madam, but I think it would be in order to
arrest this man.'

'It's not a man.'

'What?'

'I do wish you hadn't turned up just now, Colonel.'

'It looks as though I turned up just at the right
time.'

'Oh dear.' The tone of Albright's double had
changed, and it now sounded like resigned
schoolteacher's. 'I can see there's no arguing with you.
Excuse me a moment, will you.' The impostor withdrew
a small mobile from his breast pocket and told it, 'I'm
going to move one or two people. Key in the co-
ordinates to somewhere relatively safe, will you.' A
voice in the other end spluttered something in an
unidentifiable language. 'No, no, comfortable - with
plumbing. Make it snappy. One of them wants to
arrest me.'

'What is going on?' demanded Albright.

'I'd rather not think about it.' All the same, Diana
went into the hall where she pushed on a comfortable
pair of shoes and collected her and Julia's coats.

'I am sorry about this,' announced Albright's
double. 'We don't have any choice, you see. It's best you

don't report back and persuade several battalions to hunt us down when they could be doing better things, and we like to keep human beings out of matters as much as possible.'

'Meaning,' explained Diana, 'we might start to complain and they would find that very embarrassing.'

The real Albright's sangfroid began to liquefy. 'Complain about what? Just what is this character up to?'

'Just brace yourself.'

'Please don't be alarmed,' said the soldier's double. 'You'll only be taken a little way from here. You'll be quite comfortable. Reniola's fitting out a place-'

That immediately quelled Diana's nonchalance. 'Reniola! Oh no! She's an-'

It was too late.

The floor disappeared and Diana, Julia, and Colonel Albright were enveloped in a semi solid mist that whirled them on the centrifugal walls of different dimensions one second, and then gently tossed them in the whipped cream of astral transference the next.

'Where are we?' The demand in Albright's voice was tinged with terror.

'I'm more worried about where we're going. Hold my hand Julia.'

'Why Mum?'

'Because, annoying as you are now, I don't want you to go and change into something else.'

'Thanks Mum. Shall I hold the Colonel's hand as well?'

'He can change into whatever he wants to.'

Not one to panic unduly, Albright felt the justification edging closer. 'What is happening to us, for goodness sake?'

'If I know Reniola, goodness will have nothing to do with it.'

'Who's Reniola?'

'Anything from a square shouldered cat to a credible impression of a barrage balloon.'

Albright's nerve almost gave out as he began to drift away. Diana seized his sleeve. Wherever she was liable to end up, she preferred to have a soldier sharing the experience, even if his sense of adventure was now hiding behind his desire for a Sten gun.

'This has to be some sort of hallucination,' Albright tried to reason. 'The atmosphere must have been impregnated with something.'

'Wait until she drops you and you can count the bruises,' Diana said knowingly.

'Drops us where?'

'I only hope, wherever it is, I can brew up a decent cup of tea and have something more than rice to cook.' Diana recalled the cellar retreat Reniola had designed for them the last time and tried to believe it hadn't been so bad, even though they were taking a little too long to arrive, which meant that the accommodation promised to be more exotic.

The stench of decomposition engulfed them and they landed on hard ground sprouting vegetation with leaves of barbed wire and stems like meat skewers. Diana needn't have brought their coats; it was hotter than a fish and chip shop in mid summer. Albright immediately loosened his tie and removed his cap, then hastily put it back on again as the sun scorched his silver hair.

Diana looked about - and didn't bother to groan. She should have known they wouldn't end up in a penthouse overlooking the Pacific Ocean. Because Titan didn't have a Pacific Ocean, it must have disorientated Reniola. Wherever they were, it was certainly tropical and, apart from the barbed wire bushes, had plenty of ferns. There was even wildlife; in the distance herd of large animals was grazing. The heat haze rippled the view so much that it looked as though those huge bodies on thick legs were munching away at the horizon. The occasional head loomed up on a neck like the stem of a picked tulip, as though sniffing the air. A trumpet of alarm spasmodically burbled across the plain then died away as though losing interest, and the grinding of gizzard stones carried on unabated.

Before they could work out where they were, something huge thudded its way towards them on hind legs as powerful as the hydraulic rams that used to raise Tower Bridge. Colonel Albright didn't like the way it moved or how the Sun's rays caught the saliva drooling from its massive jaws.

As there were no tanks to call on and King Kong wasn't going to block its way, the soldier drew his revolver.

'I don't think that peashooter would be much good,' Diana advised.

'Why not?' Albright was beginning to wonder if his dependability as a soldier was of any value at all.

The creature headed towards them at quite a turn of speed for something carrying at least seven tons.

'That's Tyrannosaurus Rex!'

CHAPTER 13

Salisbury and Yuri arrived at Diana's back door the same time as Eva and Honey Paymaster. The four of them took it in turns to hammer the knocker and ring the doorbell. There was no response, so Eva climbed in through the open window over the sink and, after stepping into a bowl of cold washing up water and knocking several saucepans from the draining board, let the others in.

They searched the house.

'That's very odd,' said Honey. 'I watched Colonel Albright come in. His car's still outside.'

'I don't like it,' Eva announced. Being the most realistic of the group she had already assumed that something diabolical had happened.

'Can't we send out a search party?' suggested Salisbury.

'They've vanished, man.'

Yuri became agitated. 'But to where? How could they? Who could have-' He stopped as he remembered the fake Albright. 'You say the real Colonel Albright arrived?'

'Yes, I told him what was going on and he came over on the next plane,' explained Honey. 'Now there's no Atlantic, it didn't take very long.'

'Oh well,' sighed Eva. 'Somebody should take that hired car back. I've got the feeling they'll be a fortune to pay on it by the time we see them again.'

'Why you say that?' Yuri demanded, even more agitated.

'You know damn well.'

'What I know?'

'You two had better tell us.'

Salisbury turned pink in embarrassment at the thought of sounding such an idiot.

Yuri wasn't so reticent. 'That Albright - he was not soldier.'

'I assumed as much,' said Honey.

'He was really super entity made of pure energy.'

Honey's expression froze.

Eva gave a smug grin. 'There, told you didn't I.'

'Go on?' Honey managed to ask.

'He was really creature called Dax.'

'Dax and Reniola were the two cosmic "intelligences" who stranded us on this midget planet,' Salisbury felt obliged to add as he sensed incredulity fill the small living room.

'Well,' said Eva. 'What sort of explanation were you expecting?'

'I'm not sure,' muttered Honey. 'We can't go back to the beginning can we?'

'No time. This explanation is as good as any other, and I'm inclined to believe it myself.'

'What about Colonel Albright and your friends?'

'He was armed?'

'Only a service revolver. You know how tricky they still are in this country about people carrying guns.'

'I don't see why they should have been so worried when they once had a planet that could disarm continents.'

'Where could they have gone, though?'

'Yuri?'

Yuri shrugged. 'These creatures do not say much.' He stopped guiltily and looked at Salisbury. 'Do you think that Moosevan ..?'

Salisbury became rigid. 'No, I will not try to talk to her.'

'She try to talk to you.'

'Why should she know anyway? Why should she tell me if she did?'

'She fancy you.'

The two women glanced uneasily at each other. They didn't really want to know what the men were talking about. It obviously hinged on some deep emotional confusion they mutually shared, probably to do with middle age passion and why they didn't have enough of it between them to cope with the same girlfriend.

'You contact Moosevan,' insisted Salisbury. 'Now you're no longer sober she might fancy you again.'

'I not chase any woman. I do not like them any more.'

'Oh no? I've seen the way you look at Diana, or shouldn't I mention that in front of Dr Hopkirk?'

'She is only wife, and pays rent.'

Eva shrugged disinterestedly, and Salisbury

rounded on Yuri. 'I'm not surprised Moosevan went cold on you. You have the morals of a neutered alley cat with a good memory.'

'What you mean?' snapped Yuri.

'I mean, it's about time your body told your libido to stop giving Diana the eye.'

'That is not true! You are jealous because you want Diana.'

Salisbury blushed. 'How - how dare you!'

Having scored a bull's-eye, Yuri looked as though he was about to go into a celebratory dance. There was hardly enough room to hand jive, so Honey and Eva slipped out into the back garden to let the argument rumble on. They had the feeling they might find out something more useful once night fell and they could look through a telescope.

CHAPTER 14

The two men argued themselves out and, like adolescent boys, fell into deep discussion by the time evening came. As they paced round Yuri's cottage, turning over all the other useless plots they could think of to trace Diana and Julia, a short, dapper figure stepped from nowhere.

They stopped dead.

'Colonel Albright?' muttered Yuri unsurely.

'Is this the person?' demanded Salisbury.

Yuri felt uneasy. 'This is one of them.'

'I'm sorry about all this,' Albright announced genially. 'There was a bit of a foul up, you see. I forgot how bright Diana could be. She went and rumbled the ruse before I could get her to help me with Moosevan.'

'This is fake Albright.'

'Sorry about that as well. Didn't think the old boy would find out so soon.'

'What you do with Diana and Julia?'

'Oh, they've quite safe. Reniola's looking after them.'

'Oh no,' Salisbury groaned.

Yuri snarled with rage. 'Now look, you, Dax...'

'Don't be annoyed. I thought of something else instead.'

'Something else? For what?'

'Well, it's like this, you see. We need to speak to Moosevan. She won't talk to us, though.'

'Why you need to talk to Moosevan?'

'It's just a little idea we worked out to rectify your planet's problems. We have to let her know about it ... just in case.'

'Just in case of what?'

'Oh don't let's go into that now. May never happen.'

'Knowing you, it is certain to happen.'

'Let's just say, we have to contact her.'

'You expect us to co-operate now you've spirited away Diana?' snapped Salisbury. 'Of all the infernal nerve!'

'We don't want you to do anything dangerous.'

'We've heard that one before.'

'It will be totally safe.'

'And that.'

From the depths of Yuri's addled brain a spark of common sense briefly glimmered. There was no way they could win a contest with these creatures. 'What do you want us to do?'

'Well, you both know Moosevan still fancies you.'

'No, we did not,' he lied.

The counterfeit Albright went on regardless. 'I'm sure you wouldn't object to humouring her a little.'

Salisbury and Yuri looked at each other and silently agreed that they would.

Salisbury's manner stiffened. 'Will you bring Diana and Julia safely back if we do it?'

'Of course.'
'What does it involve, then?'
'Just a little trip out to see the old girl.'
'And you will bring us safely back if-' Salisbury
suddenly registered what the alien had just said.
'What? You mean ..?' He tried to point to the Earth and
Yuri helpfully realigned his arm in the right direction,
'... out there?'
'Where else, old thing.'
'This sort of travelling is not good for digestion,'
Yuri advised. 'They take all molecules apart and fire
them through space. This way they go round
gravitational corners and travel faster than light.'
Salisbury swallowed hard. 'How?'
'No mass.'
'Molecules have mass.'
'Not way they break them down.'
Unable to maintain her pretence any longer just to
humour the two men, Dax pulled a fob watch from a
uniform pocket and glanced at it. 'Optimum time will
be in about five minutes, otherwise it'll have to be
straight through the sun.'
Salisbury was quite indignant. He preferred to
believe that someone with his intellect would have
taken at least a couple of hours to argue round. 'You
thought you could persuade us in only five minutes?'
'Well, time is time, you know, and we can't do
anything without Moosevan's approval.'
'We have been trapped,' Yuri declared. 'We cannot
refuse.'
'I think I'd like to.'
'I think I can drink half bottle of gin in three
minutes.' Yuri started back to his cottage, but his legs
no longer belonged to him.
'I'll put you down somewhere you used to know,'
they could hear Albright's voice say as infinity
prematurely swallowed their protesting molecules.

CHAPTER 15

The Dringle surreptitiously checked that its side arm was on maximum charge as it disembarked from the ship after Kulp. The Olmuke had hidden the back-up portal on a planet that was uninhabitable and the gully where it was located looked as though it had been narrowly missed by several meteorite strikes. The Dringle knew nothing about the engineering needed to make the gravity corridor operational and hoped that Kulp could activate it before Krykal arrived to collect its promised meal. Unpalatable morsels they might have been, but anger can be a remarkable suppressor of the taste buds.

Despite everything that had happened to him, Kulp set about restoring the portal with an enthusiasm that would have withered in anyone else eons ago.

As it knew it would be a long time before it was able to sleep soundly again, the Dringle went back to contemplating the chances of hitching a ride on the first passing cargo freighter. Unfortunately, with an entity like Krykal in the vicinity, no shipping would dare enter that sector, so it sat and watched Kulp. If it survived, this was certainly going to be the last time it helped some megalomaniacal, paranoid genius of an Olmuke to escape.

With the aid of the ship's robots to do the heavy work, Kulp brought the portal round to operational mode. Violet light streamed from the circular barrier. In its centre, time and space were contorted and compressed until images from different dimensions reached out from the bottomless anomaly.

Something writhed into existence and made a snatch at Kulp. He stunned the tentacle with his blaster and sprayed the portal area with several volleys to deter any more intruders.

The Dringle was horribly fascinated. It didn't realise that there was a universe even uglier than the one it inhabited and hoped Kulp didn't expect it to follow him through the portal. Wherever he had managed to locate the other end of the gravity corridor, there was no guarantee of a return ticket.

The Dringle kept very quiet in the hope Kulp would forget it was there. Then the sensor he had been told to watch beeped.

Krykal had arrived.

With the speed of someone who loved life, the more humdrum the better, the Dringle dived for cover beneath the hull of the space ship. This was one of the best moves it had ever made. The ship was constructed with such dense material the lightning entity hardly registered its presence. But then, Kulp was the one it was interested in.

The green engineer locked in the portal's co-ordinates to planet Earth. Krykal descended and spread itself in a pulsating layer above their heads. They were probably the first mortals to see the creature without its planetary armour; shrunk to a fraction of its true size and blazing with a terrifying intensity like a galactic virus looking for a star cluster to bury its fangs into.

Kulp smiled to himself. There was no way Dax and Reniola could defeat this creature.

CHAPTER 16

Colonel Albright stood gazing with a mixture of annoyance and disbelief at the prehistoric predator pounding towards them. He would have needed an armoured division to halt something that size.

Diana and Julia didn't have the tactical brain of a soldier and knew more about self-preservation. They seized Albright's sleeves and ran. Were the two adults 20 years younger, and the teenager ten years older, they might have managed to keep well ahead of the lumbering mobster bellowing for their rapidly coursing blood.

'My teacher said the tyrannosaur couldn't run any faster than five miles an hour because it was too heavy,' panted Julia.

'Well, if it doesn't eat you, you can tell your teacher he was bloody well wrong!' Diana shouted at her.

Albright was beginning to flag. 'Perhaps we could climb a tree, or something?'

'It's taller than any bloody trees around here!'

'I can't keep this up.'

'I told you you shouldn't have come in.'

'How was I to know I'd end up being chased by a thundering dinosaur?'

'Stop wasting breath and run!' screeched Julia.

Diana suddenly stopped dead. 'I've got an idea.'

The only thing that prevented Albright panicking was exhaustion. 'Can't you have it and run at the same time?' Diana didn't move. 'What is it, for pity's sake?'

'Split up.'

The Colonel wondered why he hadn't thought of that. 'Good idea.'

He darted off to some sand flats, cocking his gun as he went and unaware of how much practise she already had with situations more frightening than this one.

Julia charged straight on and Diana veered off towards a swamp. Not having a brain large enough to entertain three trains of thought at once, the tyrannosaur hesitated. To help the creature make up its mind, Albright fired a couple of shots at its thick hide. The creature looked puzzled and quite offended. Then it became annoyed.

'Mum! Mum!' screeched Julia. 'It's chasing the

Colonel!'

Diana stopped in her tracks and turned towards a small cliff that dissected their paths. The ground was firm, so she was able to dash up it before Albright was underneath. The top was littered with rocks that the sun had obligingly cracked into handy chunks. As soon as Albright had staggered past, she pelted the oncoming dinosaur's head with every rock she could lift.

Julia ran back to her mother with screeches penetrating enough to make a pterodactyl turn turtle.

Though the rocks spun away from the creature's skull like wine corks, they reminded it of how annoyed it was. Head height with the top of the cliff, the tyrannosaur made erratic snatches at mother and daughter with jaws that could have crushed a tractor. Julia was at the age when young people begin to have aggravated feelings about reality and felt a little cheated because it never moved like a computer generated animation. If it didn't sound like East Enders or look like CSI, it couldn't be real and had to be an illusion her mother had created to wean her away from the television.

Several rows of dagger like fangs clacked together and narrowly missed the hem of the schoolgirl's skirt - perhaps it was real after all.

'Shove a stick up its nose Mum!'

'Don't be so bloody silly! Look and see if the Colonel got away.'

Julia darted out of range of the jaws to peer over the edge. 'He's fallen down, Mum. Looks like he's fainted.'

'Oh shit!' Diana hurled a rock with such force the tyrannosaur swallowed it.

'I'll go and help him.'

'Don't you dare!' Diana screamed, but it was too late.

Julia dashed down to the foot of the cliff and took the revolver from the unconscious soldier, and carefully examined it. There were times when watching vigilante films paid off. It seemed to be loaded and cocked. Julia tossed sand over Albright to try and camouflage him, and then dashed back up to her mother.

Diana was beginning to find the exertion of hurling rocks too much. 'What have you got there?'

'It's all right, Mum.'

'You silly little prat!' Diana jumped back as the jaws made an uncomfortably accurate snatch in her direction.

Before she could stop her, Julia darted as close as she dare, pointed the gun at the tyrannosaur's open jaws and fired several shots. Though it had a digestive tract capable of coping with most things because it seldom bothered to chew anything, small pieces of hot lead presented something of a problem. The animal was more used to having the bones of its prey lodge in its teeth, bullets it wouldn't be able to pick out so easily.

Mother and daughter apprehensively stepped back as they heard a bullet being crunched flat. The small evil eyes turned on Julia as though about to tear an explanation from the schoolgirl, then the other bullet lodged in the roof of its mouth reminded the creature she was holding the weapon that had fired it.

The dinosaur retreated a little.

'I hope that doesn't mean I've interfered with time?' Julia declared with true Doctor Who concern.

'Interfered with time? Sod that!'

Warily, still keeping its eye on them, the tyrannosaur backed away and wandered off to scavenge something for supper instead.

'How's the Colonel?' asked Diana.

'I think the heat got to him.'

They were about to dash down when another
dinosaur with a ridiculous waddle ambled up the slope
towards them. In its scaly arms it carried the
unconscious Albright.

Julia raised the pistol.

Diana knocked the weapon down. 'I'm going to sort
this one out,' she snarled.

'Eh, Mum?'

Mum didn't answer and strode towards the 25 foot,
mauve, duck-billed hadrosaur as though she were the
one as tall as a two storey house and the dinosaur an
extension about to be demolished.

Whatever skin she wore, no creature could quite
manage to look like, 'Reniola!'

'I say,' said the hadrosaur. 'I'm frightfully sorry
about all this...'

Julia gawped. 'Uh?'

'No one hurt is there?'

Diana stammered with rage. 'I'm going to, to, to...'

'It was an accident, just a silly accident. I had this
nice little penthouse on some island off Fiji all made up
for you before I remembered that there weren't any
Pacific islands on Titan, so I transferred you to Earth
instead. Somehow managed to mix up the time
coordinates. Could never get the hang of time, you
know. Usually left that to Dax but, as you know, she's
always too busy to bother helping me.'

'You realise we were nearly chewed up by that
thing!' Diana stabbed a finger in the direction of the
puzzled tyrannosaur skulking near the swamp.

'Oh, I shouldn't think so - they usually spit most of
their food out. Something to do with the way their jaws
are hinged - all right going up and down - side to side
gives them problems-'

'Reniola!' roared Diana. 'This isn't funny!'

Reniola gave her a beaky smile. 'Have to think
about the wildlife, you know.'

'Even those things?'

Reniola put the Colonel down. 'Don't worry about a thing. Make everything right in a jiffy.'

'Mum ..?'

'What is it?' Diana snapped irritably.

'That dinosaur can talk.'

'Yes dear, now go and find a nice stegosaur to play with.'

Reniola thoughtfully looked the soldier over. 'Not much damage done. Just heat exhaustion.'

'What's a stegosaur, Mum?'

Albright groaned and came to. He saw the concerned expression of a huge mauve dinosaur looking down at him. 'What the-?'

'How are you?' it asked patronizingly.

He had no sensible answer. 'Don't suppose you've got a cup of tea have you?'

Reniola turned to Diana. 'There, I told you. It's only heat exhaustion.'

Diana folded her arms and looked as uncooperative as a vixen about to jump out of a gamekeeper's sack. 'Well, what are you going to do about it?'

But Reniola had turned away to admire the scenery. 'Nice view from up here.'

'Wonderful, if you like the wildlife armour plated, and vegetation like razor wire.'

'Can't send you back just yet,' she apologised. 'Dax is using the transmission beam.'

'On who?' demanded Diana.

'Should be "whom",' corrected Julia.

'Remind me to take you to the next PTA meeting and get someone to adopt you.'

The hadrosaur flapped its arms. 'Nothing to worry about, nothing to worry about at all.'

'If you don't intend evolving into a bird, stop fluttering like a demented dragonfly and do something about this heat.'

'Of course.'

Without warning a huge sunshade sprouted from the hard ground. As well as casting a huge shadow, it was brightly coloured enough to attract the attention of every predator in Gondwanaland.

'We are also thirsty.'

Up sprang a table set for tea.

'Coo, Mum. Cream cakes.'

Mum was far from satisfied. 'I am not sitting on a rock.'

Several padded wicker chairs appeared.

With Julia's help, Albright pulled himself up and viewed the scene. Still very shaky, he toppled into one of the chairs.

'How about something to see off the wildlife?' he asked.

Reniola thought for a few moments, and then produced out of the thick, malodorous air, a small red box. She handed it to Albright.

'What the devil is that?'

'Frequency alarm. Just push the button and it will assess the danger and send out a signal to warn off whatever it is. All to do with how developed their eardrums are.'

'I'd prefer something with a trigger.'

'Oh, goodness no! This is a conservation zone. Be no end of trouble if we start seeding prehistory with 21st century bullets.'

Julia hid the gun under her cardigan.

'How long are we expected to stay here?' demanded Diana.

'Not long, not long at all. Just long enough for us to-' Reniola snapped her beak shut.

'To what?'

'Nothing you need worry about. Take no time at all.'

'Can I have a cream cake Mum?'

'Yes,' growled Diana.

With an absurd daintiness for fingers more adapted for grubbing up roots, Reniola wielded the teapot and poured her resentful guests a cup each. Albright watched, stony-faced, reluctant to believe his own eyes and relieved he wasn't contemplating memoirs. He knew a general who was, and wished he could join them.

'You should put the milk in first,' Diana chided, and then hesitated. 'Where does the milk come from anyway? There can't be any milkable mammals in this place.'

Julia smelt the jug. 'It's probably the sap from some sort of latex tree, Mum.'

Reniola thumped down the teapot. 'Milk is not compulsory. Would you like to know the bush the tea leaves came from as well?'

Diana shook her head. 'I'll pass before I become totally paranoid.'

Careful not to let her cardigan fall open and reveal the revolver tucked in her belt, Julia put sandwiches on plates. As she handed the Colonel his, she pushed the weapon back into his holster. He fingered it gratefully, having never believed any gun could be so reassuring. Albright belonged to the school of thought that suspected firearms only provoked aggravation, but realised that trying to reason with a Tyrannosaurus rex was not even worthy of any idea that might have crossed the brain which a brontosaur kept up its backside. Trying not to show it in his expression, he also wondered whether this talkative hadrosaur was monopolising a few molecules that would have been better helping some primeval amoeba evolve. They may have been primitive, but at least made pretty patterns. Reniola looked like an inflated mauve sack. Even her crest lurched this way and that as though it were the carelessly tossed on helmet of a

Viking who had missed his longboat.

Diana sensed that Albright was pondering over the embarrassing enigma of Reniola and was relieved he was trying to work it out for himself so she wouldn't have to explain it. Julia was happy to accept that they had been catapulted back several million years by a garrulous dinosaur. As long as it supplied cream cakes she would remain as compliant as a mesmerized rabbit. If Reniola was able to produce a television as well, she would go through the school's library and amend all the libels committed against dinosaurs - what did all those busybodying palaeontologists know, anyway?

Reniola gave one of her satisfied, bovine grins. 'It's very nice to meet you again like this - but I have to get on. Few measurements to take.' She turned to go, her tail almost up-ending the table.

'You mean... you're going to leave us here?' complained Diana. 'The sun's about to set.'

'Oh, don't worry. I'll come back and make sure you have some dinner.'

Reniola waddled off and Diana let out a screech of rage.

Albright looked rather sheepish and Julia, wearing a moustache of cream, paused to gaze at her.

'I don't suppose it would help if I was to say I was sorry about all this?' Albright suggested.

At that moment, Diana was ready to fight anything that so much as whimpered. 'What's it got to do with you? That creature has always been an incompetent lunatic.'

'This wouldn't have happened if I hadn't barged in. I get the impression I was really the one they wanted out of the way so my double could carry on doing whatever he was up to.'

Diana's blood pressure suddenly decided it was too mature to hurtle about her system at the speed of light, and she slumped down at the table. 'Don't worry about it. If I know anything about those two, we're better off stranded with herds of prehistoric predators than back home.'

'This is really home, though, isn't it Mum?'

Julia was right. They were at least back on Earth, albeit during a rather inconvenient part of its history.

Diana looked at the setting sun and wondered out loud, 'In that case, why are there two rather massive moons rising just over there?'

CHAPTER 17

Eva persuaded Honey Paymaster not to report Colonel Albright's disappearance. The astronomer knew that it would only complicate things to have a UN unit descend on them at that moment. Instead, the two women gathered up the previous night's observations and went to Yuri's cottage.

The cover was still on his reflector. That meant that it hadn't been used: he was usually to tipsy by the time he had finished observing the eccentric goings on in the sky to put it back on. Ominously, the back door was open and the brisk morning air was purging the smell of their last meal from the kitchen. Rapidly Eva searched the bedrooms. There was no sign of Yuri or Salisbury.

Honey sighed. 'Oh dear, Eva, I hope all the people you know don't have the habit of disappearing like this?'

'It's bloody inconvenient. I'm pretty sure Yuri would've made some sense of those observations.'

'What could we have done about it if he had?'

'Lodged a complaint with God, or whatever's meant to be in charge of this idiot Universe.'

'I doubt you'll find a cathedral to accept it now the fundamentalists are in charge. The names of God and

Mother Nature are no longer to be taken lightly.'

'Oh, don't start.'

Honey recognised the tone well enough to know she should have ignored Eva, but her nerves were beginning to jangle like wind chimes in a gale. 'What do you mean, don't start?'

'I've always known the human race were a load of ignorant bigots. There's no need to tell me about it.'

'You wouldn't really care if we were all swept away by the Black Death, would you? Whatever did this to us, not only left the bees, they also left us our fleas, you know. There could even be a new strain of smallpox if the chemists aren't allowed back into society, not that there are any animals to experiment on.'

Eva had other matters on her mind, and the last thing she wanted at that moment was an argument about a plague infecting a world where humans sort refuge from the wicked, wide Cosmos in their narrow preconceptions. 'Do give it a rest. Santa Claus never existed either. Everything was always bullshit.'

'You do realise that the pro lifers have now got the power to stop experiments on human nail clippings if they wanted to?'

'So what? Whoever removed the wildlife at least left us a few bacteria to eat the rubbish.'

'If those bacteria exist, so must others. We will die of a virulent disease lurking in the plug hole before anything astronomical takes a swipe at us.'

If there had to be an apocalypse, Eva preferred it to be cosmic. 'Why should all calamities have to be domestic? Why can't humans come to terms with the fact that disasters happen?' Eva mimicked Honey's light American accent. 'Momma, Papa, Easter Bunny, and apple pie could as easily be struck by a comet as the Sahara Desert. And, after the Earth started to think for itself then made off with all the wildlife and

left us on this midget world, it's liable to make a bloody
big impact.'

Honey was annoyed into an icy calm. 'So, what do
we do about it?'

That caught Eva off guard. Like most people with
a good line in complaints, solutions didn't come so
easily. 'There must be some way-out transcendental
group who could make contact with those super-beings
Diana and Yuri knew?'

Unfortunately it would have taken ages to find any
likely candidates. The register of religious movements
was now a complete mess: the UN could only keep
track of those who wanted to exterminate the others
for blasphemy or turn them into pumpkins.

Eva sighed. 'At least we haven't started to eat each
other yet.'

Honey took an ominously deep intake of breath
and the smile she had inherited from her Polynesian
mother vanished. Eva wasn't inclined to ask why.

CHAPTER 18

Though it would have taken the threat of sudden death
to make them admit it, Salisbury and Yuri were glad of
each others' company. The Earth Dax had sent them to
no longer resembled the world they had known. There
was something unnaturally mellow and Victorian
about the hazy landscapes and strategically placed
copses and ponds. It was less Capability Brown, more
like the background for a cottage scene in a Mrs
Miniver film; the sort of vista you would expect to find
dotted with stone angels and wisteria archways.

Yuri hoped they had only arrived in an atypical
patch, and he led Salisbury out of the small garden full
of jasmine and bad-tempered robins in the hope of
finding a few thistles and dandelions. Unfortunately,
whatever else she might have been inconsistent over,

Moosevan was sure about the way her planet should look. Before them lay more mismatched pastel vistas, vibrant patchwork meadows, embarrassed looking cattle and, although Salisbury didn't believe his eyes, even after he had put his glasses on, a giraffe making its lanky way through a herd of puzzled red deer.

The smaller animals tended to see Yuri and Salisbury first and hid. Because the two men didn't appear to be a breeding pair, they hoped this meant that the Earth wouldn't be overrun by humans again. They already had enough trouble coping with natural predators and finding their own food. All the sheep that had once been domesticated now monopolized the lush meadows like drifts of cotton wool moving over a viridian carpet. Those herbivores sensitive to intense colours tended to opt for the milder olive and sap green leafscapes of the woods. Grassy glades that would have been grazed away by rabbits were preserved by the liberal number of foxes, stoats, and feral cats patrolling them. Every now and then prairie dogs poked their heads up from their tunnel mounds and wondered what they were doing in this misty, damp landscape.

The beavers didn't mind; there was plenty of running water and trees to fell, and they had the ancestral suspicion that they once belonged here anyway. So did the wolves, but as there were so few of them, they felt outnumbered by their lunch. When meat on the hoof came at you in a wall of bleating off-white wool and didn't realise that it was meant to panic, the momentum somehow went out of the chase. These carnivores remembered what had happened to members of the pack who had managed to escape before - they had usually been lobotomised with a bullet: it was safer back in their enclosure at Whipsnade Zoo.

'Do you think this is England?' asked Salisbury.

'I do not think it is Australian outback, but Moosevan, she has little taste and not too much colour sense.'

'I hope this is England.'

'Why is this so important?'

'I'm not one for travelling abroad much.'

Yuri thought for a moment. 'Do not worry. I think we will not be able to catch ferry anyway.'

'She's certainly made a picture of the old place, hasn't she.'

'Yes - painted by colour blind Pre-Raphaelite and berserk Monet.'

'I wonder what the animals make of it?'

'I think it wise not to ask. Moosevan prefer to ice cake. There can be nothing left of rugged wilderness. Siberia is probably now alpine rock garden and Australia sectioned into flower zones like Battenberg cake, glaciers smoothed down at poles and sprinkled with glace cherries and hundreds and thousands...'

Salisbury tried to picture the prospect. His expression was suspiciously enthusiastic. 'I wonder if she has filled in the Arizona Crater?'

'No doubt Grand Canyon as well, and Sahara overgrown with Christmas trees.'

Salisbury sighed. 'I suppose you ought to try and get her to speak to you.'

Yuri stepped back as though about to fall down a hole. 'Me? Why me? You were last boyfriend.'

'I'm not sure how to go about it.'

Yuri shrugged. 'You just clear your mind and... concentrate.'

Salisbury didn't like to admit that his sensitive disposition hoarded so many phobias and fancies, clearing them away would have been like trying to chip the ice off the Eiger. 'You try first. It will save time.'

Yuri gave a wicked laugh. 'You do not want to look fool in front of squirrels.'

'Personally, I couldn't give a damn if a herd of woolly mammoth were watching. I just think that you are in a better state of mind to tackle this than I am.'

'Oh, so you think you are rational one, then?'

'I didn't say that.'

'You have fancy education and always wear tie. I am foreign and do not drink port - that's what you mean.'

'Well, as you brought the subject up, you are a total mess.' Salisbury knew that Yuri was acting out of character. His behaviour didn't bother him, so much as the reason.

The astronomer watched Salisbury's lanky frame stride off to where he could contemplate a curiously purple horizon streaked with yellow clouds.

Yuri sat down, cross-legged, where he was and thought.

A hedgehog poked its nose from under a pile of leaves to find out if it was dark enough to get up, saw the Russian trying to beam his addled thoughts into the ether, and poked its nose back. There didn't seem to be as many snails and worms as there once were, and now some transcendentally minded human had turned up to frighten off the beetles as well.

Yuri's brain, still reasonably anaesthetized by gin, slipped gently into slumber mode and laid itself open like slate quarry waiting for a troop of monkeys with a sack of chalk. There was the flickering of something large and ponderous, though he was unable to tell whether this was Moosevan or due to hardening in his cerebral cortex. Salisbury watched him warily in the hope he wouldn't have to assume the same position and look like a guru with a back problem.

Yuri lifted his head a little as he felt a stream of empathy, albeit a very sluggish one; Moosevan thought on a different time scale. The frightening exhilaration he had known when first encountering her flowed through his body. It was like being scooped up by Ezekiel's chariot and spun on wheels within wheels - all plugged into the same socket as a thousand fiery angels. The ecstasy made Yuri topple over into a deep sleep.

Salisbury wasn't sure what to do. Having no first aid kit and little knowledge about brain haemorrhage, he flustered a little and did some fervent wishing. Like a bad fairy coming to collect a good tooth, the fake Albright was suddenly standing before him.

He smiled agreeably. 'Well, did he manage it?'

'If he ever comes round he might tell you.'

'Oh, looks like it. Jolly good.'

'Look,' said Salisbury petulantly. 'If it's all the same to you, I would prefer it if you dropped the silly accent and uniform. We both know you're an impostor.'

Dax was a little crestfallen. 'Oh, I rather liked being saluted.'

'Well, there's nothing else on this planet that could raise two fingers accurately enough. Why was it necessary to assume that persona for our benefit anyway?'

'Would you have listened to me if I'd grown six pairs of wings and descended in a whirlwind like the Metatron?'

'Of course not, I'm a rationalist.' Salisbury looked dubiously at the comatose Russian. 'I can't speak for him. He has never said anything rational and seems to be on speaking terms with Baba Yaga. Perhaps if you'd arrived in a house on chicken's legs or in a flying cauldron he might have paid attention.'

Yuri looked strangely content in his slumber. This annoyed Salisbury. It was comforting to know everyone else was feeling the same when he was confused and annoyed. What right had the man to be enjoying himself?

'Can't you do something to liven him up?'

'Like what?'

'How about changing into something alien enough to give him a fright.' Salisbury added hastily, 'As long as it doesn't give me heart failure.'

Dax sighed. Unlike Reniola, she had a sense of the elegant and thought any garment or skin that didn't have that just ironed look, bad taste. Slimy, slithering creatures were out and it had to be something with a crisp outline and precise movements. There was one alien entity which could fulfil those requirements. Bringing all the components together in the right order could be tricky...

Salisbury gave up trying to rouse Yuri and sat down.

Eventually the astronomer spluttered, swore, and laughed to himself before opening his eyes to face cruel reality. 'I think I -' But he saw the figure behind Salisbury, and let out a squawk of alarm.

Salisbury turned. Behind him was a slender alien encased in gleaming crystals. It looked like a lamppost wearing a suit of polished diamonds, had an unhuman expression and as its eyes moved they spangled the scenery with the colours of the spectrum. It gave Salisbury quite a turn as well.

'What do you think you are now?' he snapped.

Dax's new persona was not nearly as amiable as Albright's. The soldier's mouth may have been tight, but this creature didn't have one. Its words sounded like vibrations trying to find their way out of a cavern of stalactites.

'This is a silicon life form from a little known planet on the tip of the spiral arm of your galaxy.'

'Well, do you have to glitter so much? It's in very bad taste.'

This rankled. 'I suppose you would prefer Reniola to design you a wardrobe again?'

Salisbury paled. The last effort that entity had

made to clothe the scholar had inflicted him with recurring nightmares about crushed soft fruit and an old tweed covered armchair one of his professors had in his study. Legend had it that the jam stains on its arms were really blood. Salisbury, even as a student, didn't possess an imagination lurid enough to work out how else they might have come about.

'I was merely making the point that now is not a convenient time to have a flock of magpies descend on us.'

Yuri interrupted. 'I think I hear her.'

This immediately stopped the debate about galactic fashion.

'What did she say?' demanded Dax.

'I am not sure. She bother about lightning for some reason.'

'Lightning? Why should Moosevan bother about lightning? She can make her own thunder storms whenever she wants.'

'I do not think this normal lightning.'

Coping with the humdrum concerns of an everyday planet and a partner with time incompetence had distracted Dax from realising something of cosmic importance.

'Will she talk to me?'

'She say you always mess things up.'

Dax tinkled with annoyance. 'Well, there's gratitude!'

'Look,' said Salisbury, 'now we've managed to contact her, how about rescuing Diana and Julia from whenever they are and letting us go back home.'

'Well, if she won't talk to me...'

'That's hardly our fault.'

'You'll have to reason with her.'

'Why not tell Yuri what you want to know?'

Dax retreated a little. 'Ah, that might not be such a good idea.'

'How you know I want to know what it is?' Yuri scolded. 'It is probably something to do with us all dying horribly.'

'Well, we can't stop here indefinitely,' protested Salisbury. 'There must be wolves and brown bears wandering the woods, and what do we live off?'

'Magic mushrooms,' said Yuri.

'You may want to spend the rest of your life inebriated, but I -' Salisbury checked himself, aware that the schoolteacher in him was beginning to show.

Like the class rebel, Yuri scoffed, 'You want to see every detail and hear every snarl of whatever is about to devour you.'

'I have no intention of being devoured.' Salisbury could hear his voice growing unnaturally loud. If he had used those tones on his more truculent students he wouldn't have needed to consider going to a therapist for dented teachers. 'This situation has become quite ridiculous. The only reason we agreed to come here was to make sure Diana and Julia were safely returned. We did not agree to play at being messengers for lunatic aliens who have too much trouble arranging their own molecules to be trusted to shunt anyone else's about.' Yuri was smiling blissfully. 'Now what's the matter with you? You look like a Siberian cat thrown out of a lorry in mid smile and freeze dried.'

Yuri knew what he was pleased about, and he certainly wasn't going to admit it.

CHAPTER 19

Feeling refreshed and a little more confident with a revolver in his hand, Colonel Albright inspected the immediate area before the sun set and Reniola returned with dinner. He just hoped it wouldn't be braised brontosaur, or worse, some other dish he needed to shoot first.

The soldier sensed that many lurking creatures
were trying to size up whether he was edible. The
nearby swamp was glutinous, bubbled a lot, and its
stench, which was an amalgamation of putrefaction,
boiling tar and bad eggs, was strong enough to stand a
spoon in. Albright stubbed out his cigar just in case the
gas was explosive then went to investigate a copse
rustling with excited movement. Gingerly he pulled
the fronds aside. There were a couple of creatures that
must have escaped fossilization because he had never
seen the like in any book on prehistory; they looked
positively friendly, like huge embarrassed rodents
caught out in some intimate act. Perhaps they hadn't
survived because they were so coy about mating, or
needed to get in more practise. Albright allowed the
fronds to fall back into place.

As he returned to Diana and Julia, he relit his
cigar to purge the foul smell of the swamp from his
nostrils and had the sudden fancy that the Hound of
the Baskervilles was bounding after him from the
steaming morass. He refused to look back and satisfy
the stupid thought.

Diana had hardly found anything more interesting
to do to pass the time. She was trying to paint her
fingernails with some varnish she had found in the
pocket of her daughter's coat before the heat hardened
it, and Julia sat looking resentfully into the distance,
wondering how many episodes of the current soaps she
was going to miss because of this stupid excursion. All
the hours she had spent trying to convince her school
friends that she belonged to a well balanced, one
parent family with a mother who was far saner than
local gossip would have it had been pointless. Now she
was faced with having to admit what had really
happened or pretend once again that she had been
visiting her cousins' ecologically aware family on the
coast. The first option would have led her to a child

psychiatrist's couch, and the second associated her with a green movement that had been taken over by fanatics who worshipped Mother Nature and battled religious fundamentalists trying to resurrect the Spanish Inquisition.

Colonel Albright wasn't the stern soldier many thought lurked beneath his amiable exterior - he was apparently reasonable all the way through and had been retained to deal with civilians instead of being pensioned off before reaching his mid-fifties. There had been many armies before Moosevan started to rearrange the Earth and none of them capable of coping with its consequences. Confronted with being abducted to prehistory by some confused intergalactic entity, most other men would have panicked or prayed. Colonel Albright fastened his tunic and stubbed out his cigar on the shell of a creature too long deceased to know anything about it.

By the time he returned, Julia was watching an extraordinary television with an aerial complex enough to pick up TV channels being beamed from the Magellanic Cloud. Despite this it was, given the choice of any channel in the Galaxy, tuned into a programme of mind numbing tedium observing the slow motion trauma, death, and decomposition which went into laying down a coal seam. Diana had long since lost the equanimity to be able to endure such boredom and was checking under the lids of several dishes to make sure that whatever Reniola had put under them was stationary. There appeared to be nothing toxic or undercooked.

'I won't need the revolver after all, then?' Albright asked.

'The curry seems to be the liveliest thing.'

'In this heat - I'm not surprised.'

Reniola had assured them that the air would get cooler come nightfall and the wildlife would slow down.

Something massive swooped low over them and the sunshade flapped.

'Dratted pterosaurs. They've been doing that all evening,' complained Diana.

'Must be the colours of the umbrella.'

She ladled out their meals and Albright handed a plate of food to Julia.

'Thank you.' Julia's gaze didn't move from the screen.

'Ignore her,' whispered Diana. 'She never takes anything in unless she sees it on television first.'

Albright sat down at the table. 'There's some pretty gruesome stuff on that one.'

'You should see one of the soaps she watches.'

Diana pointed to a door in the rock face beyond the screen. It was a conspicuous orange and, in case that wasn't noticeable enough when the sun went down, had a luminous, baroque handle. Reniola had supplied them with a bathroom, a cupboard with clean laundry, and a washing machine, though Diana wasn't inclined to use anything that ran off swamp gas.

Albright wondered what they were going to sleep in. They were bound to be oak four-posters with embroidered curtains and casters which would roll their occupants into the nearby swamp as soon as the twenty four hour sundial Reniola had provided struck midnight. It would probably be safer to stay awake all night, or sleep in the laundry cupboard with the door locked.

Albright pulled out his tin of small cigars. 'Do you mind? I don't smoke that often, but find it helps me think.'

Diana wondered why he wanted to think about the situation. 'I'll have one as well. This stench is beginning to get me down.'

'Let's hope there isn't too much methane in the atmosphere.' He struck a match and lit their cigars.

'Smoking kills at least three thousand people every year,' Julia observed as the TV screen showed yet another innocent grazing animal being sucked into the rapacious pitch bog.

'And you'd be surprised at the number of children who die before their fourteenth birthdays because their mothers had run out of something to smoke.' Diana noticed Albright's bemused expression. 'Do you have children?'

'A daughter. She not only hides my cigars, but the brandy and whisky as well.'

Diana was on the verge of asking about his wife, and then changed her mind.

Albright wasn't so reticent. 'I hope your husband won't be too alarmed at you disappearing like this?'

Diana gave a tired laugh. 'I'm an unmarried mother.' Albright involuntarily raised an eyebrow. 'We come in all shapes and sizes,' she added.

'Oh, I beg your pardon. It's just that you looked somehow...'

'Married? I know. If I knew what it was that made others think that, I'd do something about it.'

After eating as much as they dare, Albright and Diana sat back to watch the red sun set like a hot air balloon plunging to earth, and listen to the odd gurgling and slurping from the nearby swamp. The sky had hardly darkened when the light of the two massive moons sent an eerie, pale hue over the landscape like badly spotted cosmic super troupers, creating shadows where they would have preferred it to be illuminated.

Albright yawned and wondered what Reniola was up to before realising it was a better not to know.

Diana turned to Julia. 'Isn't it about time you switched that thing off?'

'Oh Mum, it's only up to the late Permian.'

'We can take it in turns to sleep.'

'I'll stay awake.'

'I've no doubt you could, but I'd prefer it if you watched for predators instead of the television.'

Suddenly the screen went dead.

Julia was furious. 'What happened?'

Albright yawned again. 'Probably needs another ammonite in the slot.'

The table and the remains of the meal vanished and a double bed sprang up in its place.

'Reniola!' roared Diana.

'Sorry,' sang out a disembodied voice.

'He's a respectably married man!'

The double bed turned into three singles.

'Actually,' Albright corrected her. 'I'm a single parent as well.'

'Oh.' Diana was too tired to enquire how he had managed it.

'I think your daughter should sleep in the middle.'

'She snores.'

'I don't!' the teenager screeched.

The Colonel smiled. 'Oh well, might frighten off the animals.'

Diana examined the beds. 'I'm not happy about this.'

'It's marvellous sleeping under the moon - two moons.'

'I've never been on manoeuvres.'

'They tried to make me stay at base, though I did manage to get out sometimes.'

'Stay at base? Didn't you ever command any troops?'

'Only volunteers.'

'Volunteers?'

'The UN regulars thought I was trying to get them killed because I arranged exercises with catapults instead of firearms.'

'Sounds dangerous?'

'Helps sharpen the reflexes if you feel vulnerable.

I've only carried the revolver since ecology started to turn somersaults.'

Having bounced on all three beds, Julia declared, 'I want the one in this end. It's soft.'

'All right,' agreed her mother. 'It's your back.'

Albright got up and stretched his legs. 'I'll take first watch.'

'Oh no! Reniola brought us here; she can make sure we aren't eaten in our sleep.'

There was the thud, thud, thud of weary footsteps as a three ton hadrosaur plodded up towards them.

'You're safe enough,' announced Reniola. 'If some predator or other comes up, you just have to ignore it. It'll soon lose interest.'

'Only if we can look at it through a sturdy fence.'

An enclosure of titanium stakes shot up.

'No chance of us getting back to our own beds is there?' asked Albright.

'I've nearly finished. Just be patient.'

'Only this atmosphere is beginning to get me down. I'm sure our lungs aren't designed to cope with it.'

The one where they came from wasn't much better and Reniola thought it best not to tell them how toxic the prehistoric air actually was. Had they known about the minor adjustment she had made to their respiratory tracts, they would have probably complained about that as well.

Diana flopped onto a bed. 'Oh, let's get some sleep.'

'Well, aren't you going to bother with the nightdress I designed for you?'

'Reniola.'

'What is it?'

'Go away.'

'Thank you all the same,' added Albright, not wanting to think about on how he would look in pink, frilled pyjamas, 'I prefer to keep my uniform on just in case there is an emergency.'

Reniola sneered like a Cretaceous Lady Bracknell.
'Emergency! What possible emergency could there be?'

'Well,' said Diana. 'Even if that tyrannosaur doesn't have night sights, there could always be an earthquake, and I've no doubt the lava in this place can flow uphill; I don't know what insects have evolved here, but I bet a few of them carry germs more deadly than malaria; there are plenty of recent craters about the place that could have only been caused by meteorites...'

Albright took up the onslaught. 'I also suspect that some slimy, indestructible, and very hungry creature will lurch from that lake of pitch at the stroke of midnight - something's already gnawed half way through the umbrella pole.' He kicked it and there was a furious squeaking and scrabbling of claws. 'Those two moons are no doubt capable of reflecting enough ultra violet to bleach beetroot stains out of white cotton, and I would feel a lot safer with a contingent of heavy artillery at the foot of my bed.'

'Is that all?' asked the indignant Reniola.

'No,' said Diana. 'When did vampire bats evolve?'

'About the same time as homo sapiens,' Reniola replied huffily, and plodded off, straight through the fence.

CHAPTER 20

The Dringle willed its metabolism to give off fewer vibrations than a hibernating hedgehog while Kulp tried to point out to Krykal that he couldn't operate the gravity portal until the entity loosened its stranglehold on him. Only now did the Olmuke have serious misgivings about risking his gleaming green skin so a few nouveau riche could have holiday homes. Then he began to panic; whenever he stopped thinking about money, he knew he was losing his grip.

'How long will this take?' demanded Krykal.

'The portal's already open, but if you insist I go through as well, I have to adjust the gravity to compensate for my atomic structure. It's nowhere nearly as dense as yours. Of course, I could always wait here if you wanted?'

'You will come with me.'

In his panic, Kulp's concentration lapsed and allowed in a disturbing thought - Krykal was communicating with the same mental link as a planet dweller, so the murderous entity must have been closely related to those creatures. Somewhere in evolution's past, one had opted for a quick nutritional turnover, and the other a quiet, interminable life. The criminal wasn't sure whether this revelation was comforting or not.

Krykal at last released Kulp so he could feed in the necessary computations to transmit his Olmuke physiology through the portal and hope that the Dringle, wherever it was hiding, wouldn't tamper with anything when he was gone.

At last the tunnel through time and space to a distant galaxy was safely open. There was nothing else for it; Kulp would have to go first and risk that Dax and Reniola wouldn't be waiting for him before Krykal caught up.

CHAPTER 21

For all the bizarre fundamentalist beliefs and commitment to the Great Mother Earth, it started to occur to some humans that it was becoming more difficult to breathe. At least with good old photochemical smog you could tell what was poisoning you. Now they realised that this insidious decline could only have been explained by all the scientists they had driven underground.

As the atmosphere continued to thin, someone suggested that scientists should be persuaded out of hiding, even though most of them were well beyond bothering whether their species survived or not. There would be little comfort from science; no physicist was going to put their head above the parapet to explain that human beings were, after all, only so many grains of sand being churned in a cosmic ocean oblivious of their existence. If people really wanted to keep their self esteem, they were better off with their self-justifying religions - better to perish as a martyred believer than self-confessed nonentity.

CHAPTER 22

Salisbury probed about the undergrowth in the hope of finding a mushroom. Dax could have easily provided Yuri and him with a menu if either of them had bothered to ask, but now she had decided to look like a diamond merchant's showroom, they wouldn't have trusted her to know the difference between a toadstool and ten-course banquet. At least, here on Earth, the air smelt fresher than it had for centuries and there were no petty officials to charge them with trespassing or picking wild flowers. Perhaps they shouldn't have been so reluctance to return. There was a lot to be said for the Earth, even if Moosevan did have a skewed idea of Laura Ashley colour coordination.

All the same, Salisbury was bothered that Yuri now seemed to be suspiciously agreeable to the situation. It was obvious the astronomer knew something Dax and he didn't in the way he behaved as though he had just won a duel over a beautiful lover. As the thought crossed Salisbury's, mind he dropped his stick in the lemon coloured nettles. Of course! That was why he was being so smug - Moosevan had returned her affection to Yuri, her old sweetheart.

Inexplicably, Salisbury found himself wondering what he had done to put her off. True, he hadn't shown much enthusiasm for her romantic attentions, yet that was hardly surprising. The idea of girlfriends hadn't crossed his mind for years and he resented being suddenly hijacked by one the size of a planet. But what else was bothering Moosevan? He watched Yuri lounging amongst the buttercups. What could any female have seen in him? His hair was like a deranged dandelion clock, his legs were so short they barely reached the ground, his clothes would have been rejected by a hypothermic scarecrow, and his English was so terrible it was amazing some mighty entity like the planet dweller would want to probe his thoughts. Never having been jealous of anyone before, Salisbury didn't immediately recognise the sentiment. It had a peculiarly bitter taste.

Only after he had admitted it to himself did Salisbury realise that Dax had left; that dull charge in the air that sent the wary toad and pine marten scurrying, was no longer there. Then, as though to revitalise the men's interest in her, Moosevan worked a little magic.

As Yuri lay dozing, a tree shot up from the ground beside him. Salisbury immediately forgot about mushrooms as its branches burgeoned with mangoes, bananas, cherries, three types of apple, and several citrus fruits. If the scholar had been his normal, apprehensive self his reaction would have been that most of them were out of season. However, appetite overruled caution. Though Moosevan would have probably bent its branches down so Yuri could reach the fruit, Salisbury quickly picked enough for both of them.

Yuri vigorously pulled the peel from an orange. 'I think this is what Eden was like.'

Salisbury scrupulously checked his fruit over

before peeling it as though something was liable to
lurch out and bury its fangs in his fingers. 'Well let's
hope she doesn't decide to create you a gin fountain.'

'What is matter? You not like out-of-season
strawberries?'

'There were probably maggots, even in Eden.'

Yuri lolled back. 'Ah, you do not trust her?'

Salisbury's eyes narrowed. 'You know damn well
you're the one she fancies now. Why shouldn't she
poison me?'

'Moosevan does not harm people - unless you are
Olmuke of course. Even then, rocks she drops on them
are only small ones.'

Salisbury froze. 'I wish you hadn't said that.'

'What is matter?'

The don shook his head. 'No - it isn't possible.' He
took his glasses from his waistcoat pocket and put
them on. 'It's all right. I must be seeing things. If he
had decided to come back to this planet there's no
reason why he would have landed just here - wherever
here is. Though Dax did say something about putting
us down near a place we had -' Salisbury stopped
before he convinced himself that they were near the
site of Kulp's original portal.

Yuri allowed juice to run down his chin as he
realised what the scholar was talking about. 'You are
hallucinating.'

'I hope so. Otherwise geography is going to be in
for a hammering again. My eyes have never had a
problem with green floater, though.'

Yuri wiped away the juice with his sleeve. 'Why
should Kulp come back here?'

'I don't like to think about it, but I bet it would
have something to so with what Dax is up to.'

'Kulp cannot be here,' Yuri insisted before he lost
his appetite.

Salisbury mouthed the words to himself as thought

trying to convince his subconscious. Not knowing what Dax had done with the Olmuke the last time they all parted company didn't help to set his mind at rest. He laid his handkerchief over his trousers and warily began to peel a banana. 'I wonder what Diana and Julia are up to?'

'Diana, she has called Reniola many names by now.'

'Well, at least they've got a soldier with them.'

'He is too old to be much good, and no taller than me.'

'He must have brains to be a colonel.'

Yuri shivered. 'I should have brought jacket.'

'Funny sort of breeze,' agreed Salisbury.

'Has Dax come back?'

'Feels like a storm brewing up.'

'But sky is clear?'

'Would that bother Moosevan if she fancied having a storm?'

The two men finished their meal and went for a walk, neither admitting they felt too scared to stay where they were with the prospect of Kulp prowling about. Self preservation is a stronger instinct than jealousy and, without the umbrella of Moosevan's affection, Salisbury didn't allow Yuri from his sight.

Neither knew where they were. Apart from purple tints in the horizon and streaks of cloud clinging to every peak like strands of well whirled candyfloss, Moosevan had totally relandscaped the place where Dax and Reniola had routed the invading Mott androids. Perhaps the men were holding the alien entities in too much contempt after all. Given what they had achieved, they should be entitled to get just one thing wrong.

Unfortunately, Dax and Reniola had got several things wrong, and one of them was darting through the decorous copses and hedges a short distance behind them.

Kulp should have felt secure in the company of a lightning entity capable of devouring Moosevan, but didn't. Firstly, her powers had increased after being transferred from her original planet and to the larger Earth; secondly, he didn't know where Dax was; thirdly, he was convinced that Krykal was just as likely to devour him.

Salisbury stood and marvelled; he had never seen lightning creating a blazing curtain across the sky before.

Nor had Yuri, and he had involuntarily spent more time in isolated places nearer the North Pole than Salisbury.

Instead of going to earth, plasma was rippling about the sky as though looking for some massive wok in which to stir fry a few meteorites.

'It says something about fiery dragons in the Anglo Saxon Chronicle,' observed Salisbury.

'I would sooner meet fiery dragon and all its relatives than this.'

'Shouldn't think Moosevan will allow it to hang about for long. Or perhaps she decided to cook up the display?'

'That is not natural - not even for Moosevan.'

'How do you know? Is she talking to you?'

'She can sense great danger.'

'What sort of danger?'

Yuri became agitated. 'We must contact Dax.'

'How? We don't know where she went to.'

'This isn't electricity. It is entity. It is dangerous to Moosevan.'

'How could anything be dangerous to Moosevan, for goodness sake?'

'It is predator.'

'Of planet dwellers?'

'Of anything with energy.'

'Just as well I'm not feeling very full of life at the moment.'

Salisbury's circumspect response to the prospect of being barbecued along with the rest of the planet lathered Yuri into a rage. 'You are myopic, soft-brained nincompoop!'

Salisbury gave a teacherly frown. 'Steady with the long words, you might suddenly start speaking English.'

Yuri knew that Salisbury was only getting his own back for something. He wasn't bothered what it was at that moment. 'You are English teacher who defends punctuation; I am astronomer who knows when Cosmos is becoming dangerous.'

'Why get into such a tizzy? There's nothing you can do about it, so you might as well save your energy.'

Yuri did just that. He folded his arms, turned his back on Salisbury, and tried to ignore the tingling in the roots of his hair that had been given more shocks than they could cope with. Eden didn't seem such a good idea after all.

He eventually sighed. 'I wish Diana was here.'

'I'm rather glad she isn't.'

'Then who is to rescue us?'

Salisbury suddenly stiffened his resolve as a though he had once captained his college's cricket team instead of only supervising the tea urn. 'Pull yourself together, man.'

'If I had ever pulled myself together I would now be seven feet tall. I think Dax would hear us better if we panic.'

Salisbury was determined to ignore Yuri's warning, even at the risk of being turned into a six foot sparkler. 'You're being ridiculous. What possible danger are we in?'

Yuri suddenly had that mind numbing sensation of déjà vu. The lightning would have to wait its turn.

The two men turned very slowly and saw the large splayed feet and grotesque green expression of an Olmuke.

CHAPTER 23

Eva and Honey once again ploughed through the observations of the night before. There could be no doubt - something was juggling with their solar system and whatever was doing it seemed rather inept. If the moons and asteroids the astronomers had been watching remained on the same trajectories they would collide in a collective centre of gravity.

'What is going on?' muttered Honey, now prepared to admit that those who existed in the comfortable worlds of Momma, Papa, Easter Bunny, and apple pie were about to receive a fright of cosmic proportions .

'Planet building,' Eva declared too enthusiastically.

'There won't be the mass for another Earth. It would take another body the same size as our moon - Earth's moon that is. I need to contact HQ.'

'Your team must have already spotted it.'

Honey looked apprehensive. 'Perhaps not.'

'Why not?'

'Our observations were being targeted by some religious fanatics. The astronomers have probably boarded up the telescopes and left. The only reason you haven't been picked out so far is because you're next to an architectural museum and trashing antiquities would set the preservation fanatics at their throats.'

That ugly thought had briefly crossed Eva's busy mind. This was the time to be in an observatory on top of a mountain surrounded by jungle. She looked at the radio telescope array looming over the museum of architecture. It was still counting wavelengths.

'Shut them down, Eva.'

'I can't. They're committed for years ahead.'

'How many astronomers have been calling in for results?'

Eva had to admit they hadn't even been able to interest the Press Association in the last supernova. Reluctantly she reached for the phone. 'Fiona, we're going to shut down the array... Yes. Now. I'll be down as soon as I've finished here.' Eva turned to Honey. 'What do we do now, for pity's sake?'

Honey had her chin balanced on fingers that almost appeared to be in prayer. 'How's your profile?'

'What d'you mean?'

'One of us will have to go on television and explain a few things before that new planet starts to take shape.'

Eva knew that it wasn't going to be her. 'Don't be daft. You'd be lynched.'

'People will panic if we don't.'

'Let them. They've got in enough practise to be good at it by now.'

'Don't you care what happens to the human race?'

Eva had always believed humans were the mistake of some interfering entity. 'Nature probably regards us as the slug that accidentally slipped into its evolutionary pot of jam.'

'We're not slugs, Eva.'

'Did you give up your car to save the next generation?'

Honey opened her mouth to protest that no one else had either, and then realised Eva was baiting her. 'Did you?'

'Why should I? I've always been a self-centred slug. I leave a trail of slime every time I walk up the High Street with all the other molluscs.'

'What are you driving at?'

'If anyone from this solar system is going to explore the rest of the Galaxy, I think it would be best if it were not us.'

CHAPTER 24

Considering their predicament, Diana and Julia slept well. When they woke, breakfast had been laid out on a table for them.

Grateful to be spared the sight of a massive, mauve duckbilled hadrosaur in a pink flowered apron wielding a frying pan, Diana cautiously approached the coffee. It smelt like coffee, was probably filter and the milk made art deco scrolls over its inky depths. She handed a cup to Albright who looked as though he had suffered nightmares for all three of them. Julia swallowed two glasses of orange juice and became annoyingly perky. Diana followed her old routine of tossing cornflakes into a bowl, then slopping milk over them. Before cows had disappeared, it had given her a perverse satisfaction to see the golden flakes slosh out of the bowl and lay in a sodden heap on the kitchen table. She had originally done it to deter Julia from the habit. Now Diana had somehow never been able to break the pattern, in the same way she used all the swear words she had cured her daughter of bringing home from school.

Albright looked on benignly, no longer surprised at anything.

'Ignore her,' Julia mouthed.

He gave a tiny nod of agreement for fear of attracting retribution.

After eating, they tidied themselves up. Julia somehow managed to will the prehistoric television back on and planted herself in front of it, while Albright suggested tentatively that they look for Reniola. Diana thought they should know when they were well off so, from their vantage point, they watched the lumbering wildlife munching away at the scenery, while smaller bipeds darted here and there to snack on insects.

Albright sighed. 'Think of all the information we
could take back to the palaeontologists if we only knew
what to look for.'

'Weren't they abolished a couple of weeks ago?'

'Were they?'

'Well, the only biologists and zoologists allowed
now are the fundamentalist ones. You know, Big God
made all this - hang whether it's rational or not, but
He is our God.'

'Oh yes, of course. Palaeontology wouldn't suit
them at all, would it. Pity Reniola couldn't send back
that tyrannosaur. That would have cramped their
doctrine a bit.'

'It would be your troops who had to bring it down.'

Albright knew how well a platoon of his volunteers
armed with catapults would cope with that. He gazed
intently at the horizon. 'Oh look, that moon's rising
again.'

Diana rubbed her eyes. So it was. How odd. She'd
heard about a similar phenomenon on some other
planet, but couldn't remember which one Yuri said it
was.

Albright was unsettled. 'Shall we take a little
stroll?'

'Why not.' Diana tossed Julia the small red device
Reniola had left them. 'Use this if anything comes up
here.'

'What about you then?'

'I always thought you wanted to be an orphan?'

'I've plenty of ammunition,' said Albright. 'We
know their soft points now, don't we.'

'Reniola says it's a conservation area,' the teenager
reminded him.

'You can see if that thing has any effect on her as
well if you want,' Diana told her, but Julia had
returned to the interminable story about the making of

a coal seam. Things were getting interesting - there was now quite a deep layer of peat ...

'Have you ever watched the grass grow?' Diana asked Albright as they walked down into the valley of grazing herbivores.

'Often thought I might like to. Old brain won't let me, though. I'm one of those cantankerous souls who will die totally aware of everything about them, including what did it.'

'I'm finding it more and more difficult to act my age as well. Must be something to do with the calcium and evening primrose.'

Albright would have suggested that it was more likely because of the company she kept if he hadn't been so much of a gentleman.

A triceratops ambled across their path. Albright reached for his revolver.

'It's all right, it's vegan,' Diana told him.

'What could it eat to get to that size, for goodness sake?'

'Jungle a day perhaps.'

'Cavalry of those would make the enemy think twice.'

'You wouldn't command it though, would you?' she suggested mischievously.

'What makes you say that?'

'You've never shot anything in your life.'

'I would have brought that tyrannosaur down if I'd had a bazooka.' Then Albright admitted, 'Recoil would have probably flattened me as well. Come to think of it, I am safest behind a desk. Had to join up, though. Family tradition. Younger brother into the Church, another into Whitehall, and older sister into politics.'

'She's an MP?'

'Yes, ran some campaign in the European Parliament to stop pro lifers banning women from having periods, or some such hogwash.'

That gave Diana a start. 'What?'

'Don't understand it myself. Something to do with them wasting the potential of a human egg.'

'You sure you've got that right?'

'Probably not. I get muddled over those sorts of things - female plumbing and all that. She had to go underground anyway since the fundamentalists took over. Has to keep out of the way of those neighbourhood vigilante groups who go about looking for little old ladies to accuse of witchcraft, and little old scientists to accuse of heresy. Joyce is a tough bird, though. She should have joined the tank corps, and I should have been a clerk in a gentlemen's' outfitters.'

Diana laughed. 'With your brain?'

'Not been much use so far? I should have shot myself in the foot or pretended to be a transvestite.'

'Not much good in a gentlemen's' outfitters...'

'I always wanted to have a try at being kinky, but everyone else was doing it in the 60s and 70s, and by the time the 80s came I was past it. Apart from that, I had a father who court-martialled a corporal for allowing a C.N.D. protester to put a carnation in the barrel of his gun when on guard duty at some nuclear submarine base. Man got his own back, though. Think he became a spy for Cuba... or something very Graham Greene.'

'How did you manage to have a father like that?'

'Mother was a marvellous woman, just no judge of men, only bloodhounds. She bred them, you know... Placid old beasts, bloodhounds. When they start baying, it can get to you after a while...' Albright made an effort to stop rambling. The place was obviously disorientating him. It must have been the atmosphere.

'Funny that tyrannosaur never came back,' noted Diana.

'After what your daughter did to it, I don't think so.'

'Yes, she's not exactly Little Miss Muffet.' She hoped Albright's sister, Joyce, won her campaign. Having periods might bring Julia down to the real world... whichever one it was.

There was a thud as though a mountain on the other side of Pangaea had suddenly decided to go for a stroll.

Albright stopped dead. 'What the devil was that?'

'Try not to think about it. There's a probably a perfectly irrational explanation.'

'Do brontosaurs stampede, do you think?'

'If Reniola's offered to design them pinafore frocks, quite probably.'

Albright nodded and tried not to think of paisley patterned dinosaurs.

The occasional pair of eyes watched accusingly when the couple passed, as though aware they had something to do with the mauve hadrosaur and her bleeping box. A pterodactyl the size of a DC 10 swooped down on them. Albright fired a couple of shots over its crest and it caught the next thermal to glide off.

'It's getting too hot,' said Diana. 'Think we ought to start back?'

Albright nodded.

As they turned, he stared with disbelief into the distance. 'What the devil is going on over there?'

'Where?'

He pointed at a whirlpool in the sky. It could have been a climatic effect, though more likely had something to do with Reniola. The landscape looked as though it was being drawn into a funnel and whirled around, tornado fashion.

'Definitely Reniola,' decided Diana.

The whirlpool gained height. Suddenly it flipped inside out and shot off in the direction of the re-rising moon. Diana had a premonition about what was going to happen and thought it best not to say anything.

Then the moon disappeared.

'What's happening?' Albright asked, suspecting she had a very good idea.

'At the risk of making sense, I would say it has been sucked into another dimension... along with all the scenery Reniola had to gather up to get it going.'

The Colonel's eyebrows arched in bland amazement. 'Oh dear, I wonder where it's gone?' Diana just shrugged. He guessed. 'Oh dear.'

As the clouds that the disturbance had whipped up milled about like malevolent candyfloss, the herds of wildlife began to huddle together.

'It's going to rain.

'How can you tell?' asked Albright.

'Cows always used to sit down and, I suppose, as not all dinosaurs have a leg exactly at each corner they must be doing the equivalent.'

'Freshen the air up.' He really suspected it was going to be like a dozen monsoons at once.

By the time they got back, drops of water the size of avocadoes had started to splash noisily down on the impermeable ground and confirm Albright's worse suspicions.

'Ugh...' groaned Julia who hadn't the adult way of pretending major disasters didn't really bother them. 'My new cardigan's soaked.'

Diana watched the dye trickle through to the girl's last decent white school blouse. 'Stop complaining. Now Reniola's sorted out her little problem, she can send us back home.'

'My daughter won't believe this.' Albright sounded as though she was liable to reprimand him for being out all night.

'I'll lend you Julia to explain everything. Other children seem to understand her. How old is she?'

'35.'

'Oh...'

CHAPTER 25

Having encountered Kulp in equally bizarre situations before, Salisbury and Yuri didn't think it so odd he should turn up now.

Yuri nervously glanced at the Olmuke's sidearm. It was still in its holster, so thankfully he was there to shoot somebody else.

At times like this, Salisbury and Yuri were glad they didn't speak his language. To Kulp, human dialect was like water glugging through drainpipes, while the humans thought Kulp's speech a dribble of disjointed gurgles, and its unbroken, monosyllabic stream quite disorientated Salisbury. The Olmuke had always believed that warriors should hesitate over nothing, even punctuation, or to make themselves understood: no peace treaty had ever been drafted in their language.

Yuri pointed to the lightning blanketing the sky.

Kulp gave a salamander smile and they realised it was something to do with him.

'Think Dax knows he's here?' asked Yuri.

'I've the feeling she shot off to some other planet.'

Without warning a whirlpool formed in the lightning-riven sky's upper atmosphere.

'What is that?' asked Salisbury.

Even Kulp looked puzzled.

The three of them studied the dimensional anomaly in the heavens.

Yuri suddenly pointed 'Look, another planet! '

Salisbury put on his glasses. 'Where? I'm dazzled by that lightning.' Then he saw it; a large orb powdered with clouds hanging above the Earth like an undecided beach ball. 'Oh yes. I wonder where that came from?'

'This I do not like to think about.'

'Why not?'

'It looks like another moon.

'Is that bad? We needed another one after all. That piece of debris circling Titan isn't big enough to have any effect on the tides.'

'There are no oceans there to have tides,' Yuri reminded him.

'Oh no, of course not.'

A sprinkling of ice crystals cascaded down through the disturbed atmosphere. Yuri's astronomer's instinct to know what had happened was overpowering. His wish was tangible enough to become Moosevan's command and, without any consultation, Salisbury and Kulp were snatched up with him and hurtled in a jet stream towards the unnatural phenomenon. When they regained their wits, they found themselves in a valley surrounded by spruce covered hillsides.

'I do wish you would warn me whenever you have some whim I am liable to be involved in,' Salisbury complained.

Kulp wasn't just disorientated, he started to panic as Krykal flashed furiously backwards and forwards across the sky. Having promised the creature Dax and Reniola, Kulp now had to deliver. He drew his blaster and pointed it at Salisbury in the hope that at least one of those entities would dash to the rescue.

Nothing happened.

'Now what have I done?' the don complained. 'I always knew this creature wasn't rational.'

'Just keep walking slowly backwards,' Yuri told him. 'Put space between you and blaster.'

'What's its range then?'

'Several miles I should think. Do not worry though, I do not believe he wants to shoot you.'

'It's difficult to tell what the creature thinks behind that toad like expression. How about getting your girlfriend to do something?'

Yuri was on the verge of protesting innocence on that matter when something rather large lumbered up behind Kulp. 'You have another friend coming to help... I think.'

Without his glasses, Salisbury could see the shape, but not its fine scaly detail. 'Well, who is it? Dax?'

'No, I do not think she would walk like that, even if she disguised herself as brick warehouse.'

Either Kulp's helmet was blocking the sound, or he was too preoccupied to hear the footsteps thudding up behind him. Coyly Yuri pointed over the Olmuke's shoulder to indicate that his blaster was facing the wrong direction. Kulp wasn't going to be caught by that one. These humans must have thought, because he was daft enough to come back so Dax and Reniola could beat him up yet again that he was going to believe that those super-beings were sneaking up on him. If they were going to catch him unawares, they would have disguised themselves as something that didn't have a footfall like a succession of landslides, it sounded more like... Kulp turned.

As the slavering jaws of the prehistoric monster lunged down Yuri yelled at Salisbury, 'Run!'

Salisbury had experienced the pain of hesitating over such matters and easily overtook Yuri as they plunged up the hillside into the trees. Kulp would have done well to follow their example, but couldn't take in what was confronting him. He had encountered creatures just as large, lumpy, and ravenous in his own galaxy, but this one was not from the Earth he had come to be very wary of. Yet it had to be the Earth, because Moosevan was operating its ecosystem, so where the..? He stopped thinking about it when the albertosaurus' teeth ripped a sizable gash in his spacesuit. After blasting several volleys at the monster, he bounded after Yuri and Salisbury, not bothering to see if any had found their target.

CHAPTER 26

Diana wasn't quite sure why she found herself in a landscape filled with meadows of pastel posies and woodland of whispering beech punctuated by the occasional spruce. Despite a determined breeze rippling the grass and leaves, it looked as though it had been assembled, decoupage like, in three clearly delineated dimensions. She half expected a Hornby train to come chugging round a bend at any second.

'Now look Reniola... This isn't exactly home is it? It's Moosevan painting by numbers. Julia could mix a better palette than this.'

It was seldom her mother offered praise, so her offspring seized the excuse to tell the Universe how clever she was. 'I won a prize when I was ten. I painted a picture of a clown with powder paint and glitter-'

'All right,' said her mother. 'Now win a prize for keeping quiet.'

Opportunity to shine quelled, suppressed rebellion went up a couple of notches.

The adults were more interested in the new scenery

Albright felt disorientated. 'What sort of planet did this planet dweller come from for goodness sake?'

'It had magenta skies, orange sands, and purple trees.'

'In that case, perhaps this isn't so bad after all.' He pointed into the distance. 'What's that?'

Diana shielded her eyes and looked up. 'A table mountain.'

'What's that on it?'

'Looks like a teapot.' Diana turned quickly before Reniola could dematerialise or turn into an inanimate part of the scenery.

The hadrosaur blustered a little. 'Sorry, sorry. I forgot to clear it away. Just an after image which came through the corridor with us.'

The tea service vanished and the table cloth crumpled into a snow-capped peak.

A Yorkshire terrier darted out from nowhere and started to snap at Reniola's huge ankles.

'Oh, isn't he sweet,' cooed Julia.

'Probably rabies,' observed Diana.

Albright sighed. 'I'm beginning to think there was something to be said for Titan after all.'

'Well, I did get the time right,' complained Reniola.

'So did Big Ben before you buggered about with the calendar. I want to go back and make sure Yuri and Salisbury are safe,' Diana insisted.

'Oh well, in that case, there's no problem.'

'No problem?' echoed Albright in disbelief.

'They're here.'

'Here? Doing what?'

'Ah well...'

'Doing what?' demanded Diana.

'Well, actually, they're being chased by an albertosaurus that accidentally got sucked through the gravity corridor - But don't worry about a thing!'

Albright took out his revolver and loaded it. 'All right, where are they? And don't you dare tell me this is a conservation zone.'

'I do wish you wouldn't be so hasty.'

'Well do something about it then!' Diana shouted at her.

'Like what?'

'How about getting out of that hadrosaur's skin for a start.'

'What's wrong with it?'

'It doesn't fit you and I'm beginning to take a strong dislike to mauve.'

'This is pointless,' declared Albright. 'Are they

anywhere near here?'

'Must be,' Reniola prevaricated, 'though I can't guarantee that the albertosaurus was the only other thing sucked up with it as well.'

'So, if we see a large multi-coloured umbrella sitting over the next sunset we shouldn't be too surprised,' snapped Diana.

'They're only afterimages.'

'I'll bear that in mind when it starts to rain basins full of curry. God knows what Yuri and Salisbury must be thinking. Though, when Yuri has to run fast his brain usually seizes up...' Diana rounded on the hadrosaur. 'Just how much danger are they really in?'

'Moosevan's looking after them and the exercise must be doing their arteries good.'

'Now look...' threatened Albright.

Reniola shook her crest, 'That's funny...'

'What is?'

'There's someone else here.'

Diana instinctively knew that there one only one person who could elicit such a reaction from the super-being. 'Don't tell me. It's got to be Kulp, who you claimed was imprisoned on his home planet.'

'Kulp?' asked Albright.

'An Olmuke who gave a new meaning to "green awareness".'

'Now you come to mention it...'

'Can I see an Olmuke, Mum?' Julia demanded.

'Shut up!'

'It's mental cruelty to keep telling your child to shut-up, you know.'

Albright turned understandingly to Diana. 'This is the best part. Wait another 20 years and she starts telling you you're too senile to be interested in sex.' He turned to Reniola. 'Look, if you're not going to do anything to help the other two, you might as well point me in the right direction.'

'Don't worry,' said Diana, 'When Yuri's scared enough he can wriggle out of anything.'

Having come so close to combat, Albright wasn't going to let go of the idea that easily. 'All I need is a decent weapon and a fast Land Rover.'

The duckbill hadrosaur looked down at him, 'You aren't going to give up are you?'

'Do I look as though I'm joking?'

'All right, all right... I'll drive though.'

'What?'

Before their startled gaze, Reniola dissolved into two clouds which buzzed busily as though at work on some dimensional jigsaw. When puzzle was solved, one looked like a Land Rover, and the other a cat-like alien dressed in a natty bodice and knee pants, and covered in so much long fur it was difficult to tell where her ample proportions began and ended, She had the muzzle of an Alsatian, huge fur fringed ears like wings, bright orange eyes, and fluffy tail so long it invited her bipedal feet to trip over it. Reniola seized the swinging appendage and tucked it in her belt, only to have it somehow wriggle free and continue a life of its own.

Albright took an amazed step back. 'What on earth is the creature now?'

'She looked something like that when we first met. It wasn't on Earth, though.'

'How many planets have you been to for goodness sake?'

'Jump in, jump in,' called Reniola as she took the wheel of the Land Rover. 'Not unless you want me to transmit you there.'

For fear of her carrying out her threat, they all jumped into the vehicle without another murmur. At least this way they weren't liable to cross any more time zones or end up on the wrong planet.

'What about a decent weapon?' nagged Albright,

still not too sure about Reniola's rather wolfish persona.

'You're perfectly safe.'

'We're not shape-changing aliens who can turn into puffs of smoke every time something very large and hungry is pursuing us,' he persisted.

Reniola pondered. 'Have you thought about armour?'

'She means, as in tortoise,' Diana warned before he could commit himself.

'Well,' complained Reniola, 'What's wrong with that? They can live for 500 years.'

'I'd sooner die young.'

'You left it too late, Mum.'

Mum clipped Julia's kneecap.

'Don't worry about a thing,' protested Reniola.

'Can't you say anything else?'

'Yes, but you wouldn't like it. Hold tight, we're going over a bump.'

Julia, having perched precariously on the back of the rear seat, would have fallen out if not caught just in time by Albright.

'This is fun, isn't it, Mum!'

Diana didn't dare reply. She was looking up at the sheet lightning pulsing across the sky. Moosevan nudged her thoughts to let her know that this was no natural phenomenon.

'Reniola,'

'What now?'

'Can't you feel it?'

Reniola gave Diana a worried glance. Her passengers' hair was standing on end. Then Reniola felt her fur trying to creep out of her bodice and her whiskers begin to vibrate furiously like the strings on a flamenco guitar. No longer sure just how much control she had over her own molecules, Reniola wasn't going to admit that she was bothered and feigned indifference. 'What's the matter?'

Diana was annoyed by the entity's offhand manner. 'Don't you feel anything odd?'

'All the time. It's one of the penalties of being a hypersensitive, galactic entity.'

'How about impending annihilation?'

'Who's?'

'Yours.'

Reniola laughed, and then looked up at the lightning ominously straddling the blue sky.

She nearly turned the Land Rover over as she slammed on the brakes.

'Oh dear. So that's why I can't contact Dax.' Reniola immediately realised she shouldn't have admitted that out loud.

Diana smugly folded her arms. 'Moosevan says it's going to devour you two first, then have her as dessert.'

Albright was puzzled. 'Well, surely galactic super-beings like them shouldn't be overpowered by a few bolts of lightning?'

'That's only its visual appearance,' Reniola said knowingly. 'This creature straddles dimensions. Distant relation of the planet dwellers, you know. Quite voracious.'

'Let's find the other two first, then bother about that afterwards.'

'That's easy enough for you to say.'

'Start the engine and get going, damn you!' Albright uncharacteristically snapped.

'Will you stop giving me orders.'

In an attempt to reassert her superiority, Reniola drove the Land Rover like Rambo through an ambush towards the valley where Yuri and Salisbury were trapped.

For all their haste, they needn't have bothered.

CHAPTER 27

Moosevan had confined the albertosaurus to a large pit where it could safely rage over the way Kulp's blaster had scorched it. The most dangerous thing happening at that moment was the argument between Salisbury and Yuri about whose side Kulp was on. As he had almost been devoured by a dinosaur the last time he had threatened them, Kulp stood innocently aside as though the heated exchange was nothing to do with him. He was almost relieved to see Diana arrive in the Land Rover, but the sentiment was countered by the fact it was being driven by Reniola, one of his arch enemies. Not that Reniola was bothered by the Olmuke's presence. He had become a strange fixture in her interdimensional existence, and it would have felt odd if he didn't crop up at some time or another.

'That creature was going to incinerate us,' Salisbury shouted at Yuri.

'This is nothing. It was Olmuke joke,' the astronomer countered perversely.

'I didn't notice anything to laugh at.'

'That is because Olmuke have no sense of humour.'

'Then they shouldn't try and make jokes.' Then Salisbury saw Diana arrive.

He dashed towards her, but stopped abruptly at the sight of the long-haired entity behind the driver's wheel. Reniola's muzzle smiled. This only unnerved him more.

'It's all right,' called Julia, and pulled Reniola's tail to show how tame she was.

The entity gave a low growl. Albright took the tail away from Julia and tucked it back into Reniola's belt.

Salisbury approached warily.

Yuri made several rude gestures at Kulp, and then

joined them. Already familiar with the wolfish creature in the fancy dress, he pointed accusingly at Albright. 'That is who?'

'The real Colonel Albright,' Diana told him.

This didn't satisfy Yuri. Despite the sharp features and letterbox mouth, there was something so charismatic about Albright, it made the Russian uneasy. He was also sitting too close to Diana.

Tossing his timidity to the oddly charged wind, Salisbury threw his arms round Diana and kissed her, and then indicated Reniola. 'Just what is that?'

The question interrupted Yuri's jealous disapproval of Salisbury's chaste kiss. Knowing the creature of old, he squinted in annoyance. 'Reniola. Why she want this stupid disguise?'

'The duckbilled hadrosaur would never have fitted into the driver's seat,' Diana explained.

'How come she bring you here?'

'We were working our way home by lessening the degree of difficulty it takes her to move from one part of the Universe to another,'

Reniola's whiskers started to twitch in annoyance. 'Now look, you lot...'

'Excuse us not being more gracious, but if it weren't for you two bunglers, the human race wouldn't be in such a pickle,' Albright added.

'So what sort of saviours do your greedy, egotistical species want? Angels with snowy white wings? Bodhisattvas willing to be martyred in the name of humanity?'

'Why not?' demanded Salisbury. 'If something as unlikely as you exists, so must they.'

'True enough, but they look after the deserving cases. You muddled apes are getting all the help you deserve... and that happens to be us.'

As an uncharacteristic sparkle of malice entered Reniola's huge, orange eyes Diana felt impelled to remind her, 'Aren't you forgetting something?'

'What?'

'You're about to be annihilated.'

'Annihilated?' echoed Yuri. 'How could something wipe out intergalactic energy form - even if it is stupid?'

'I'm not listening to any more of this.' Reniola got out of the vehicle. 'I should leave you all here and let you find your own way home.' Her swishing tail escaped from her belt and bowled Yuri over.

'Probably be quicker,' muttered Diana.

'And another thing, if Dax and me are eliminated, this lightning entity will then devour Moosevan.' Reniola turned on Yuri as he picked himself up. 'So who will save you from all those wild beasts then?'

Only Salisbury could see past the acrimony to a more pertinent matter. 'But, how did this lightning entity get here? Someone must have brought it.'

Their gazes turned to Kulp. Albright was prepared to believe that the Olmuke was a bad parody of an ogre animation and it was salutary to realise that something could look even more preposterous than Reniola.

'What is that? It's too large for a toad and the wrong colour for a walrus.'

'He's the ultimate in Olmuke corruption,' Diana told him. 'They evolved that colour to reach the pinnacle of what they believed to be perfection.'

'You know him?'

Diana hummed non-committally, 'Just a minor encounter.'

'No encounter with thing like that is minor,' Yuri corrected. 'She and him save Earth from being overrun by android army.'

The feathers that could have knocked Albright down were now plentiful enough to stuff a mattress. 'Is that true, Diana?'

Diana was defensive. 'Now, don't expect me to parley with him. We don't understand a word each other says.'

Albright checked his revolver and resolved to opt for a language that knew no barriers.

'No Colonel, don't let him think you're threatening him! His reflexes are ten times faster than yours.'

'Even if you were 30 years younger,' Yuri added maliciously.

'Would he gun all of us down?'

'Only for a bounty. He's pretty straightforward when it comes to corruption and more likely to be after Dax and Reniola. They've given him a lot of aggravation in the past,' explained Diana.

It was beginning to sound like a meeting of the Olmuke Preservation Society so Reniola wrinkled her snout and pretended not to listen. True, Kulp had probably turned up to try and murder Dax and her. That didn't mean they should worry about it - he'd never succeeded before.

Albright was puzzled. 'If he's such an evil character, why did he help you save the Earth?'

'There was this army of androids-'

'Is that when you kept laddering your tights, Mum?' interrupted Julia.

'What's that got to do with it?'

'You went through two packs in a week, remember. Had to borrow mine, then when I came home I didn't have any to wear to Jill's party.'

'I bought you a new pack.'

'They were the wrong shade.'

'There was nothing wrong with them; you're the one who's the wrong shade.'

'They were a flesh shade for a pig.'

'Why not, you should live in a sty!'

Albright coughed politely, but they ignored him.

'You know I don't have any shoes I could wear

them with. You did the same thing when you bought
me that jumper.'

'They were your school colours.'

The albertosaurus in the pit bellowed with rage
and Kulp, no longer the centre of attention, began to
feel foolish.

'I didn't want to wear it for school, though, did I! '

'If you expect me to buy you another one..!'

'Why not?'

'Wool comes from sheep.' Diana pointed to the
white blanket slowly scything its way through the
verdant green of a distant meadow. 'Go and shear one
of the bloody things and I'll lend you my knitting
needles! '

'They're not the right colour.'

'What colour do you expect them to be for goodness
sake?'

'I wanted a jumper the same colour as Marion's.'

'Well go and find a pink and yellow sheep and
shear that..!'

Albright steeled himself. 'I hate to interrupt,' he
declared bravely. 'We just have this rather pressing
problem to attend to.'

'You're a parent, you should know the importance
of having to cope with a child's clothes sense,' Diana
admonished.

'It's not something that usually crosses my mind
when on the verge of mortal combat.'

'Oh, don't worry about Kulp. He'll soon lose
interest in us.'

And, sure enough, the Olmuke sidled off into a
nearby wood.

The dinosaur's roar became more deafening and
Julia told Reniola, 'Can't you send that poor thing back
home? It's not very happy there.'

Reniola had considered the possibility of it
devouring Kulp, yet couldn't think up a way of getting

him to fall into the same hole without blotting her already smudged record of non interference. 'All right. Everyone stay here. Might send out a few sparks.' She took a small box from behind one of her huge furry ears and wandered away to commit yet another puncture in the fabric of space and time.

None of the others could see what happened.

Suddenly the bellowing stopped and the dinosaur disappeared. The silence was filed with an eerie sound, like the rumbling of a million demon stomachs.

Albright sighed 'Now what's she done?'

At last Diana didn't think her child's colour sense seemed so important. 'Don't think that was her.'

Without warning Reniola jumped into the hole that confined the albertosaurus. Another figure appeared from nowhere. It glittered like a Christmas tree decorated by a pyromaniac.

'Who's that?' asked Julia.

'Dax,' said Yuri. 'I wonder when she turn up.'

'Does she know she's in danger?'

'Well, if Reniola has not told her, their communication is bad as sense of proportion.'

Albright fingered his revolver and felt redundant. 'Can't we do anything to help them?'

'Would you try to divert blast of a nuclear bomb?'

'Can't Moosevan do anything-' Before Albright could go on, several bolts of lightning struck the valley. 'Take cover!'

Everyone dived behind the Land Rover.

The ground erupted and the world about them rotated like a bizarre carousel. Trees rose and came down, roots and all, to be transplanted in a way that must have jarred Moosevan's sensitivities. Reniola's table mountain was compressed into marble as the range surrounding it closed in, and beaches were vitrified into sheet glass. The conflict was illuminated by streamers of liquid fire, which didn't do much for the vegetation either. Volleys of sparks cannoned in all directions, stampeding the grazing flocks that hadn't already fled. A sound like a buzz saw slashed across the valley, making everyone believe they were about to be decapitated.

'Why doesn't Moosevan do something?' called Salisbury.

'She's probably got her head down as well,' Diana shouted back.

'I've never seen anything like this, and I've watched munitions dumps go up,' added Albright.

'You watch H bomb tests as well,' sneered Yuri.

'No, just munitions dumps go up,' Albright insisted patiently at the top of his military voice, though he was beginning to wish for the return of the Cold War so he could intern the bad-mannered Russian.

'Stop being such a pain, Yuri,' scolded Diana. 'This could develop into something serious.'

'I think it's fun,' declared Julia. 'Just like Guy Fawkes night.'

'If you don't keep your head down we'll have to find a turnip to graft on in its place.'

'Could this thing really hurt Moosevan?' asked Salisbury, beginning to regret all the malediction he had previously heaped on the planet dweller.

'Without Dax and Reniola, what's to stop it?'

'We should kill Kulp,' Yuri declared.

'I wouldn't worry about that. Given the way it's setting about those two, it's bound to get round to him next,' said Diana.

'Why he bring it here?'

'He wants revenge on Dax and Reniola.'

'This thing will devour and devour... Look, those trees, they are nothing but burnt stumps.'

Krykal filled the valley with its luminous fury and it was impossible to tell who was winning. Eventually there came a huge, hollow sigh like heat escaping from

a furnace, the land cracked, and remaining trees
snapped. Then the conflagration abruptly stopped. The
lightning entity rolled away from the valley and into
the sky as though digesting a large meal. Unable to
evaporate, the clouds throbbed menacingly with
Krykal's presence, anchored like massive barges about
to rain molten glass.

'Stay here,' Albright ordered the others, and picked
his way down the scorched valley before they could
stop him.

'Does he always give orders?' complained Yuri.

'Go down and join him if you like,' suggested
Salisbury.

Yuri looked at the plumes of smoke rising from the
blackened ground and thought better of it.

They watched as, revolver in hand, Albright
thoroughly searched the area. He stepped over the
carbonised knolls and striations where it looked as
though a frenzied dragon had tried to claw its way out
of the Earth. As he walked, Moosevan smoothed the
ground, making it easier for him to search for the
remains of the two cosmic entities. There was nothing
left of Dax, apart from a few crystals, and the small
box Reniola had used to transport the dinosaur back
home.

The full horror of what had happened struck
Salisbury.

The super-beings had really gone.

'Pity they couldn't have turned into something
useful, like a couple of fire extinguishers,' Diana
muttered as she left the cover of the Land Rover.

'This does not mean well for either planet,' Yuri
declared.

Salisbury felt quite numb. 'Everything is going to
be stuck as it is.'

'Oh no, atmosphere on Titan will deteriorate and
humans suffocate. We will be stranded here with Kulp

and dinosaurs Reniola did not send back, and that creature up there,' he looked up at the malevolently throbbing heavens, 'will devour Moosevan.'

Julia pondered on this for a few seconds and, true to the conventions of a good soap, totally sidestepped reality. 'Just think, if Jonathan was here, we could start a whole new human race between us.'

'You couldn't even remember to feed your hamster,' Diana scoffed. 'And your descendants would end up so inbred they wouldn't know one end of a spear from the other, let alone bring home the bacon.'

'We will borrow the Colonel's gun.'

'I think he'd have to be pretty unconscious before he let you get your hands on that again.'

'Why you want to start humans all over again?' complained Yuri. 'Do not history teacher at school tell you what humans do to each other?'

'Of course. They taught us social awareness. All the girls know how to claim benefit if their parents throw them out when they get pregnant.'

'This I did not mean.'

Diana laughed. 'Here stands the child who once thought it would be a good idea to go into politics.'

'That was over two years ago. I want to be a chef now.'

'Well, you'd better learn how to use a bow and arrow.'

'That Olmuke had a weapon. I'll steal his.'

'Kulp might have been fried as well,' Yuri suggested hopefully.

Diana wasn't so sure. 'I want to see the fat and cinders in the pan before I believe that.'

Yuri shuddered a little at that revolting prospect and, as much as he wished the Olmuke was out of the way, wouldn't have wanted to see it.

Albright returned. He tossed the crystals in the air. 'All I could find.'

'I think it's about time we started to talk to Moosevan,' Diana told Yuri.

'She know what is going on.'

'And does she know what to do about it?'

'Her mind is not that quick.'

'Well, she'll have to think of something if she doesn't want to become that thing's lunch.'

Yuri gave Diana a circumspect glance. If anyone was going to do any thinking on Moosevan's account, he knew it wouldn't be him.

CHAPTER 28

Kulp was now having third thoughts about the consequences of blind greed. He had never doubted the rapaciousness of Krykal, yet was unnerved at seeing the entity in action. If it could devour Dax and Reniola, why should it bother about keeping its bargain with him? He didn't have a monopoly on the ultimate double-cross. Crouching amongst the bracken, he hoped the creature would mistake him for a moss covered rock. Kulp was able to slow down his pulse rate, though not conceal the vibrations his ego still made; Olmuke self importance would linger much longer than the life in his gelatinous blood; had he been able to switch that off he would have probably shrivelled to a mouldy looking crisp without the help of the lightning entity.

Without warning Krykal bellowed triumphantly into his thoughts, almost denting the Olmuke's skull, 'I have them!'

Kulp snatched off his helmet. Enveloped in air much fresher than he was used to, helped revive his stunned brain. When everything had stopped spinning, he wished Krykal could just whisper into his mind in the same way Moosevan spoke to humans. Given their delicate constitutions, they would have had a brain haemorrhage if the planet dweller had behaved like the lightning entity.

Kulp compelled himself to sound interested in Krykal's revelation. 'I hope they were worth it?'

Krykal seemed to hesitate. 'Perhaps.'

Although his eardrums had been dented from the inside, Kulp's wits were harder to put into shock. 'You are going to keep to your side of the bargain, aren't you?'

'I will think about it after I have devoured this planet dweller.'

'Now look...'

The creature laughed. At least, that was what the Olmuke took the sound to mean. It was at times like this that Kulp usually weakened and wondered whether he should call on Dax and Reniola to help...

What had he done? He had stranded himself in an alien galaxy with an out-of-control entity bloated with malicious energy. Kulp's brief time behind bars had made his brain soft enough to believe he could get away with such a scheme.

It was unlikely Diana would help. Even if she did have cosmic powers, she would have probably let Albright shoot him, Kulp's spacesuit was ripped so he couldn't go back through the gravity corridor and into the vacuum at its other end, and something rather large, knocking over trees as it went, was coming up behind him fast.

CHAPTER 29

Diana shook her head, unable to believe what Moosevan had just told her. Then she saw the lightning entity preparing for another strike. Collecting itself into a huge cloud that resembled pulsating magma, it rolled through the sky as though about to burn up the atmosphere. Lightning struck the landscape again and again as Krykal began to descend.

'Everyone into the Land Rover!' ordered Albright. 'I don't know what it's after this time and we shouldn't hang around to find out.'

'I'll drive.' Salisbury was at the wheel before the soldier could argue.

'I'll be rear gunner!' declared Julia, and was promptly told to sit between Diana and Yuri.

The electricity in the atmosphere immobilised the Land Rover's engine and it wouldn't turn over. So much for orders and determined action.

'Everybody take cover?' suggested Diana.

CHAPTER 30

The moon that suddenly arrived from prehistory had now slipped out of its temporary orbit and was heading towards the centre of gravity which was also drawing a collection of other moons and asteroids towards it.

***

Diana and the others had been too busy to notice, but Eva and Honey watched, transfixed, through the observatory's new reflector as the large radio telescope array was now closed down and the only power used by the reflector's drive. The astronomers took notes by candlelight and made calculations like schoolgirls who had only one more sum to solve before discovering perpetual motion. If anyone else in the world was observing what was going on out there, somewhere between the orbits of Mars and the Earth, they were also going to keep it to themselves as some, hopefully benevolent, galactic intelligence choreographed the cosmic dance. Eva and Honey would not have really wanted to know that the remarkable entities responsible had just been devoured.

Despite his previous experiences, Kulp wasn't sure whether to turn round and identify whatever what was coming up behind him or, to save time, run as fast as he could. No longer trusting his blaster to rout a whole pack of prehistoric predators, his uncompromising Olmuke nerve snapped.

As Kulp broke cover, Krykal was behaving irrationally, even for an entity that had just gorged itself stupid on the cosmic energy of Dax and Reniola. It lay like a duvet of flaming golden syrup, stabbing forks of lightning into the ground as though trying to drive Moosevan out with a thousand cuts and filling the air with the odd stench of barbecued rubber.

Kulp didn't really want to know what was bothering Krykal. Whatever it was, he was bound to get the blame ... assuming anyone survived.

The Olmuke could still hear something lumbering in pursuit. He ran back to the stalled Land Rover and checked the primitive machine over. Though there was nothing wrong with it, it was too late too late to drive away. Something voracious, vicious, and huge reared above him; a deinonychus - 20 feet of upright muscle, tendon, and teeth you didn't get on the National Health. It scythed at Kulp with the sickle-shaped claws on its hind feet.

There was a shout and volley of shots as Albright darted from cover, firing at the monster. Kulp pulled out his blaster. The enraged dinosaur knocked it from his grasp, and then leapt on the Colonel. By the time the Olmuke had recovered his balance, Albright was laying mangled in some bracken.

Another hand retrieved the blaster. With unerring accuracy, Diana fired at the sickle-clawed killer. The creature wasn't sure what to make of it at first, then lunged towards her. Diana fired another volley. This time it staggered a little; there was the evil smell of barbecued dragon and the creature toppled over.

This confused Kulp. He wasn't used to people whom he thought were out to kill him risking their lives to save him instead. Julia was first to reach Albright. Salisbury caught up and moved her aside. He soon wished he hadn't; a cut finger was usually enough to make him feel nauseous. The don nearly fainted at the sight of so much blood. Yuri felt as many of the Colonel's pulses he could find; he appeared to still be alive.

No one noticed the manic activity of the lightning entity die down. The dinosaur's powerful hind claws had ripped open several gaping wounds in the Colonel's torso. He lifted a hand as though unable to make out what had happened. Diana clasped it before he could find out.

'Keep quite still.' She turned to Salisbury. 'We have to staunch the bleeding. Find something to bind the wounds together - preferably not Yuri's shirt.'

Julia quickly pulled off her slip and ripped it into bandages while Diana unbuttoned what was left of Albright's uniform. He was in shock and needed immediate surgery. Kulp quietly retrieved his blaster and pulled its casing apart. After making several adjustments, he took out one of its small components and knelt beside Albright.

'Don't let that creature near him!' Salisbury called out in alarm.

Diana saw the pin prick of light at the end of the instrument Kulp held and realised what he was going to do. 'It's all right. Go ahead,' she told Kulp,

'You cannot trust him,' Yuri insisted,

'The only ones who could have helped him were Dax and Reniola, and they've just managed to get themselves devoured.'

'I ask Moosevan.'

'What could she do? He needs surgery, not

relandscaping.'

Ignoring the argument, Kulp, with the skill of a precision engineer, cauterized Albright's wounds. The haemorrhaging eventually staunched, Diana and Julia bandaged him as best they could with the strips of material provided by a slip and one almost clean shirt. Fortunately, Albright didn't seem to know what was going on.

'He's going to die of shock, you know,' Diana announced in a strangely toneless way as she covered him with her and Julia's coats.

'Will he really, Mum?' whined Julia.

'This isn't Tom and Gerry. People don't survive injuries like cartoon characters.'

'Shouldn't we tell his daughter?'

Yuri was standing quite still, numbed and very resentful. 'Why not Moosevan have stopped this?'

Diana gave a thin smile. 'Look at it this way; now Dax and Reniola have gone, not many other humans are going to survive either.'

'This is horrible way to die.'

'He was a soldier.'

No longer willing to try and make sense of things, Yuri darted off.

'Don't go too far,' Diana called after him but he had gone. She looked at the abashed green expression of Kulp's.

What could the Olmuke say, even if she had understood him? He reassembled his blaster and replaced it in its holster.

They sat in silence around Albright for some while. Still in shock, the soldier felt detached from their reality and imagined he was looking down from the sky at the absurd the little scene. He recalled John Gay's epitaph to himself: 'Life is a jest and all things show it. I thought so once, but now I know it,' and needed to tell the others they were victims of some huge cosmic joke. All that came out was, 'Don't fuss. It's not what you really think.'

They remained silent.

Only Salisbury, overcoming the instinct to irrationally blush, eventually managed to ask, 'What isn't old man?'

'It's all very silly really...'

Diana knew what he meant. She had worked it out for herself some while ago whilst looking into the gaping maws of that other dimension known as death.

'Are you warm enough?' Julia asked the Colonel.

'Quite. Not feeling much. Tell the green fellow he's all part of the same joke... same pond...'

'What's he on about, Mum?'

'Grains of sand.'

Diana rearranged the coats over the soldier. 'You'll be all right.'

There was little rational basis for the statement, but Albright no longer seemed bothered. He closed his eyes and drifted off into a coma. Diana wondered whether she should ask Moosevan to build a shelter over him: as long as the planet dweller didn't lower the temperature or make it rain, there wouldn't have been much point. Moosevan's idea of early autumn was a blanket of dry warm air without high winds or drizzle. Rain would probably come when everything was safely hibernating and she felt it would be ascetically pleasing to flush the pinkish blue sky with clouds.

Reniola's small box dropped from Albright's pocket. Diana picked it up and attempted to open it. Kulp took it from her and tried. Having no success, he handed it back with a shrug. She replaced it inside the soldier's uniform jacket to join the crystal remains of Dax.

Thankfully only one moon shone that night as they settled down on the mossy beds Moosevan supplied. Salisbury insisted on staying awake. He had never been able to cope with suffering, his or anyone else's, and didn't want Albright to die without someone knowing, even though the soldier would probably have the sense to do it in his sleep.

The next morning seemed a long time coming as Moosevan slowed the planet's rotation to treat her guests to a ponderous, orangish, pink dawn. She had no time for calendars, or the fact that days and nights were supposed to last a given length of time. The light almost helped to soften Kulp's jarringly green complexion as he gazed resentfully at the new sun which, with the help of a few wisps of cloud, was wearing a sarcastic tangerine smile. Diana wished the planet dweller would save her special effects for when some relation of Reniola's decided to abduct Torvill, Dean, and an ice rink.

As the sun's rays shortened, the party felt as though a web of pink sugar was being spun about them. The only one who seemed to appreciate the candyfloss spectacle was Salisbury. As soon as it was over, he dozed off to dream about the safer world of his rockery.

Albright was ominously still. Fearing the worst, Diana went to him.

To her surprise, he was breathing regularly and the silver hair had been immaculately groomed, so she assumed that Salisbury had tidied him up. Diana gingerly pulled aside the coats covering the Colonel. The damage done to his uniform jacket should have been beyond repair, but had been mended. Carefully she unbuttoned it. The makeshift bandages were no longer there and Albright's wounds had been hemmed together with rows of minute stitches.

Her gasp of surprise woke the others. They stared in disbelief at the surgery and Salisbury had the irrational fear he was about to be accused of something.

'How?' he gasped. 'I was watching all the time.'

'There can't be anyone else on the planet, not unless the squirrels have taken up microsurgery,' said Diana.

'Is he not sick now?' demanded Yuri.

'His pulse and breathing are regular and his skin quite warm. The shock appears to have worn off.'

'Perhaps we can move him now?' suggested Salisbury.

'We don't know how well his internal injuries have been put together,' warned Diana.

'Wake him up,' suggested Julia.

'He's not a hibernating dormouse!'

'Well, he's the only one who can tell us how he feels.'

'I suppose we ought to find cover of some sort in case that lightning comes back. It's kept away for so long it must be building up for something,' warned Salisbury.

'Will you go and see if the Land Rover is working?' Diana asked.

Sleepily, Salisbury tried the ignition and the engine turned over right away. He shrugged as though the woes of the Universe sat on his shoulders. Why couldn't it have done that when they needed it?

It wasn't surprising Salisbury felt everything conspiring against him. No longer wanted by Moosevan, Dax had stranded him amongst Earth's liberated fauna and flora without so much as a decent pair of Wellington boots or schoolmaster's wits.

Kulp felt he was being sucked into a marshmallow bog of human emotions, and the Olmuke in him took fright. He stayed long enough to lift Albright into the Land Rover then let them drive off to a cave Moosevan had provided. Because they had to travel so slowly they assumed Kulp was following on foot.

The entrance of the cave was in a narrow gorge

and its interior was more practical than anything
Reniola could have conjured up, with enough granite
armchairs to seat three Darby and Joan clubs. Despite
this, Yuri insisted on sitting cross legged on the floor.
If they were facing annihilation, he was going to be a
very perverse corpse.

When Albright eventually stirred, his hand
automatically reached for his revolver. It was missing.
Julia was playing with it. Diana snatched the gun
away and replaced it in the holster lying beside the
Colonel, though she doubted whether he was in a fit
state to pull the trigger, and hadn't the heart to tell
him it wasn't loaded. Now they had an alien with a
blaster, guns shouldn't be needed.

But Kulp had other ideas. No one had guessed
what they were because all his expressions seemed to
consist of variations on the same scowl. They weren't
surprised to find he had slipped away. Then those
ominous flashes of lightning crept back into the sky,
zigzagging their way over the landscape all morning,
scorching the meadows and splitting the trees
Moosevan had started to reclothe the land with.

CHAPTER 31

When the Dringle was sure Kulp and his energetic
companion weren't likely to return, it started to
explore the small planet. As the world was totally
dead, there was nothing much worth looking at, even
when the sun's glare threw its scenery into jagged
relief. The Dringle could have passed the time by
watching the faint trails left by meteors as they
plummeted down into an atmosphere hardly dense
enough to burn up a spaceship's jettisoned garbage
sacks. If it sat watching for long enough, it might well
have been struck by the compressed sewage produced
by a crew of 2000, if not a 30 ton cometary lump of iron

and exotic minerals.

The Dringle climbed back into the ship and decided to try and program a route to somewhere reasonably safe. So much for attempting to extract payment from Kulp - it certainly didn't expect to see him again. There were only enough Dringle rations to last a short while and the Olmuke idea of nutrition would probably give it stomach cramp, so there was nothing else for it; the Dringle would have to send out a call for help and take the consequences.

While it was searching for a distress frequency, the Dringle heard an odd clattering outside. It should have been impossible on a world where there weren't enough molecules in the atmosphere to carry a sound. The noise could have echoed from millions of light years away, made by something metallic crashing against the sides of the gravity corridor as it sped towards the portal. Perhaps it was Kulp... in little green pieces; the Dringle wouldn't have been surprised. It was a mistake for Kulp to make that pact with a planetful of vindictive plasma. The Dringle fastened its spacesuit and warily left the ship.

Something was coming through the portal, but it wasn't green. In the centre of the pool of violet radiation, a glittering, spinning figure materialised. The Dringle wasn't sure what to think, and there was nothing it could do about it anyway. Fortunately it wasn't Kulp or Krykal. They couldn't have made the noises that tinkled inside its helmet.

As the arrival spun like a pulsar, the Dringle decided it was time to start worrying and tried to remember the prayers to those ancient gelatinous deities its species once worshipped before the Mott declared that they were God instead.

Eventually the spinning stopped and an entity encrusted with faceted gems took shape, pulsating with light that slashed the sky.

The Dringle found the presence of mind to raise its hands in surrender with no way of telling whether this was a good move or not.

The glittering entity turned to the space-suited creature, dazzling it with shafts of illumination, raised a flashing hand and said in perfect Dringle, 'After all the gravity corridors Kulp has constructed, it's about time he learnt how to fit a bloody stabilizer.'

The Dringle didn't have an answer. Its engineering feats were limited to operating bolts and restraining delinquents with spanners, as well as its ears being filled with tinkling noises and fur.

'Not that he's going to have time to find out,' the entity went on. 'When I see him, he's going to wish he'd been genetically engineered as a subterranean mould.'

Evidently the creature knew Kulp well.

'Who... Who are you?' the Dringle asked, not knowing any silicon species with that sort of dress sense.

'I'm called Dax. It's not really my name. I stole it from somebody else. Energy forms don't usually need names - that's a mortal thing.'

'Dax...' muttered the Dringle. "I thought you were supposed to be ..?'

'Devoured by the lightning entity Kulp sent after me? I nearly was. If we hadn't known it was coming, we wouldn't have stood a chance. Well, don't stand there. Where are the controls of this portal?'

The Dringle still hadn't taken in what was happening, so Dax had to find them for herself.

Being no engineer, the Dringle eventually asked, 'What are you going to do?'

'You don't want to know, but I'd keep the engine of that ship warm if I were you. Something very large and annoyed will be coming through here at quite a lick at any moment. And I don't mean Kulp.' Dax started to dismantle the portal's control. She registered the Dringle's perplexity. 'What is the matter with you?'

'Well,' the Dringle at last admitted, 'I could get this ship into space, but haven't a clue where to point it.'

Dax groaned. 'How did you manage to get mixed up with Kulp?'

'He owes me money.'

Dax sensed what for and understood why the Dringle was reluctant to admit it. 'All right. Don't touch anything. I'll see to you when I've finished with Kulp and that dratted solar system.'

Dax completed her adjustments to the portal control then stepped into the violet radiation and disappeared.

CHAPTER 32

Honey took another gulp of black coffee. 'There's something wrong, Eva. Those asteroids aren't falling towards a common centre of gravity any more.'

'They must be. They couldn't have resisted the momentum.' Eva came over and looked through the reflector's eyepiece. 'We need that dratted computer.'

'If you had invested in a generator, you would have had enough electricity to power that as well as the telescope's drive,' Honey reminded her for the third time as she trimmed one of the candles illuminating their notes. 'It's just as well you shut down the main array before that circuit was cut off. It must have been deliberate, because the circuit in here works and I can see the street lights.'

'As long as no one knows we're here, it doesn't matter.' Eva concentrated on the eyepiece. 'You're right, there's something shepherding the asteroids into a new orbit. They're not even being attracted to that large moon.'

'Where could it have come from? There's no other terrestrial planet like it in our solar system.'

'I'm not too sure about anything any more.'

'Oh come on, if we can find Pluto, it's unlikely something over half the size of the Earth would have been missed... Eva...?'

'What?'

Honey took a deep breath. 'It couldn't be the Earth, could it?'

Eva gave her a circumspect glance. 'Only if it's had a bad enough fright to halve its weight.'

'It's got an atmosphere. Why not?'

Eva didn't want to entertain the idea. 'Probably down to whatever's been shunting things about.'

'What are they trying to do, though?'

'God knows. Looks as though the elastic of the super intelligence engineering this little display broke.'

'Oh well, at least we may not be killed by anything as straightforward as suffocation after all.'

Eva tried not to look enthusiastic. She knew that if those asteroids deviated, they could cross Titan's orbit instead.

Honey finished her coffee and absent-mindedly turned up the paraffin stove.

'Leave that fire alone. The air's beginning to ripple.'

'Sorry, wasn't thinking. I'm worried about what happened to Colonel Albright and the others.'

'They're probably a lot safer where they are. Why should you be so worried about him anyway? You're a respectably married woman.'

Honey didn't know of anything in the rules that said she couldn't do a little lusting every now and then. He was too fond of his daughter to look at another woman, anyway.

Something in the viewer made Eva almost jump. 'Oh shit!'

'What?'

'That new moon is becoming erratic as well.

Where's the last drawing we made?'

Honey took a candle and rummaged through a pile of sketches. She handed one to Eva. The moon had moved about ten degrees. They would lose it altogether if it kept that speed up, and those cracks and rills must have meant it had some plate movement.

'It's not fair, you know,' Honey announced without warning.

Eva paused to give her a long, hard look. 'What isn't?'

'Entities from some other part of space interfering like this.'

'What's fairness got to do with it?'

'You'd think someone that advanced would have a policy of non interference.'

'You live in cloud cuckoo land.'

Honey folded her arms defiantly. 'You've decided to be on the side of those entities messing with our solar system, haven't you?'

'At the rate they're carrying on, I don't think they're looking for anyone's approval.'

Before the discussion could become heated, the headlights of a vehicle pierced the darkness below.

'Hello,' said Eva. 'Looks like time for the cellar. Have you bolted up?'

'Only the front. I left the cellar's outside door open in case we had to make a dash for it.' She peered through the window in the telescope's housing. 'Hang on a minute. That's a Land Rover.

'Is that good? Ever since Daphne Trotter's horse threw her, she's been barging around in one of those.'

'No, this is UN, thank God. My text message must have got through.'

Eva gathered together the charts and stuffed them into her briefcase. 'Let's hope they don't want to know what happened to their Colonel.'

'It's all right. I recognise the captain.'

'Only a captain. I would have thought this merited a general at least.'

'Don't be such a pain, Eva. She's a good woman.'

'So was I before I met Diana in secondary school.'

The vehicle pulled up some yards away from the observatory and they heard boots on gravel crunching their way to the door.

'Sounds too heavy for a woman,' Eva said dubiously.

'She's a big girl, so don't rub her up the wrong way.'

'I've never felt the inclination to rub anything in a uniform, especially big girls.'

Eva kept the safety chain on the door and demanded to know who the visitor was. She sounded Danish and said she was a captain looking for Colonel Albright. Eva opened the door. A tall woman entered. By her blond, iceberg features, she might well have been Thor's big sister. Honey immediately sensed that Eva's annoyance at anyone over five foot six was getting into gear and quickly explained to the captain what they had just discovered, only to learn that she had a bigger surprise. NASA had crewed a shuttle which was going to blast off towards the Earth within the next 24 hours.

Eva nearly had a fit. 'Even if it's still there, that planet's no more stable than this one!'

'What do you mean? If it's still there?'

Before Honey could announce her theory about the new moon, Eva told the captain that they were unable to say where the Earth was now, and they couldn't risk a crew's life on an assumption. Those in charge had taken everything into account and still decided to find out if there was any hope of getting back to the Earth. They had nothing to lose if everyone was going to suffocate anyway.

Eva couldn't argue with that. 'So who are the lucky

few selected to preserve the human species?'

'I don't know,' admitted the Captain. 'That's not down to us.'

Even Honey's well suppressed indignation began to rise. 'What do you mean? Not down to us? Who's running this scheme for goodness sake?'

Eva soon guessed. 'All the governments able to raise the money to preserve the miserable lives of those who can pay. She gave a raucous laugh. 'I hope Moosevan likes their company.'

'Moosevan?'

'The entity that was juggling the Earth's geography before we were expelled from it.'

'She's still there?'

'I've no doubt, and I'm pretty sure she won't want to see the remaining dregs of our greedy, grasping species suddenly turn up. You tell those scheming governments that.'

'But Eva...' Honey protested. 'One or two human beings must survive somehow. Is it logical to see everyone exterminated?'

'Why not? What possible use are we to the Universe?'

The captain noticed the woman's features harden in the candlelight, and was taken aback. 'Is this the way an astronomer should reason?'

'At one time, astronomers were damned and burnt by the Inquisition, now it's about to happen again. You tell your masters what's waiting for them on Earth... if they ever manage to find it.'

The Captain gave a frosty smile. 'Okay. I'll be in touch.' She left.

Honey looked reproachfully at Eva. 'Did you have to say that?'

Eva came down a couple of gears. 'Oh yes. I believe that Diana, Julia, Yuri, Salisbury, and probably Colonel Albright, are at this moment on the Earth. If

anybody is going to survive, I would prefer it to be
them.'
<h2 style="text-align:center">CHAPTER 33</h2>

Diana and her friends weren't so sure about being on
the safest planet as flashes of lightning illuminated
their cave entrance and the ground shuddered when
each bolt found its mark. Albright was now able to sit
up and wonder if this was the same nightmare which
the sickle claw had sprung from; some sort of bizarre
afterlife, or whether his mind was going. At least his
sensations had returned and he ached in places he
thought he had lost the use of in his youth. Julia had
somehow managed to get hold of his revolver again
and, probably because there wasn't a television to
watch, was loading and unloading it as though trying
to wear out the bullet chamber.

Diana took it off her and returned it to him.

Yuri had assumed a fetal position, with knees
tucked under his chin, as though ready for
Neanderthal burial. Salisbury was subdued and
twitched nervously at each lightning strike and it was
impossible to tell what was going through his mind. It
wasn't visions of Winnie-the-Pooh or Wind in the
Willows. Diana sat on a rock shelf with her arms
folded and watched the others. She was either annoyed
or plotting. Albright pretended to doze. He should have
known better than to be curious, yet seemed to be the
only one aware that she was up to something. Even
Julia, who could chatter incessantly without a
television to watch, sat sullenly with her gaze fixed on
a crack in the rock which resembled the profile of her
Titan bound boyfriend.

When Diana was sure the others were preoccupied
in their own private worlds, she silently slipped to the
back of the cave. Albright watched keenly as a cleft in
the limestone widened to let her through. Beyond, he

could see the walls glow, lighting her way down a
passage which went deeper and deeper into the rock.
Careful not to attract the attention of the others, he
rose unsteadily and followed.

Despite the illuminating crystals in the walls, this
wasn't Aladdin's cave. It was more like the descent to
the lair of some multi headed dragon. Having had
enough of monsters for one week, Albright wondered if
he should mind his own business and turn back but, if
Diana had the stamina to make it, so would he. The
fact that he had only just miraculously survived a
potentially fatal injury inflicted by a carnivorous
dinosaur no longer crossed his mind.

Eventually Albright came to a deep chamber. In its
centre a dazzling pillar of energy rose up from the
planet's depths and struck the cave's roof. Diana was
standing before it as though deep in conversation with
the shaft of pulsating light. Even the Colonel could tell
that the chamber was filled with the thoughts of a
massive and timeless entity, thankfully, not multi
headed or breathing fire. Diana looked as though she
was listening to gossip in the local grocer's. Albright
tried to hold his breath for fear of being heard above
the silent cacophony. It was too painful and he let out
a sudden gasp. Diana appeared not to hear him so he
carefully lowered himself onto a convenient rock which
hadn't been there a moment before.

Eventually Diana raised her head. She stepped
back and the pillar of energy, with a sudden "whoosh",
vaporised the ceiling of the cave, making a wide tunnel
through the half kilometre of rock above. Although
Albright's reflexes told him to pull Diana back, the
flesh wasn't so willing. Fortunately she seemed to be in
control of the situation.

Satisfied that Moosevan had grasped the concept
of self preservation and was now prepared to put it
into practise, Diana took Albright's arm and gently

helped him back along the passage.

It was some time before Salisbury noticed that Diana and Albright had gone. On a subconscious level, he was still unable to accept that Diana had any common sense and assumed they had left the cave. In a rush of irrational bravado, the scholar darted outside into the electrical storm after them. Yuri and Julia followed in an attempt to stop him, but Salisbury had longer legs and was well away. Yuri shouted abuse in his mother tongue after the scholar and Julia screeched a lot, yet nothing would induce him to stop. Then the lightning descended in a furious, flaming curtain.

They headed for the cover of an overhang, only to find Salisbury already sheltering rather sheepishly beneath it. Yuri swore at him again. Salisbury paid no attention. He was too intent on finding Diana to worry about Yuri's opinion of him, in any language.

'Did you see them go?' asked Julia.

'No, but she must have come in this direction.'

'Why?' demanded Yuri.

'What do you mean? Why?'

'There is no reason for Diana to come out here. She is not addle-brained like us.'

'Then where could they have gone?'

'Given way Colonel Albright was, not so far.'

Suddenly this made sense to Salisbury. 'All right. We'd better get back.'

But it wasn't to be. Those sickle-clawed predators that hadn't been struck by lightning, or cooked by Kulp's blaster, had detected the distinctive aroma of panic. Before Yuri, Salisbury, or Julia could move, a semi circle of the slavering creatures cut off their escape.

CHAPTER 34

His spacesuit no longer functional, the lightning's charge in the atmosphere was having an oppressive effect on Kulp's Olmuke physiology. It didn't help when the creature causing it suddenly demanded a conversation.

'What is it?' said Kulp. 'What's bothering you now?'

'You tricked me,' Krykal's voice resonated it his head. 'How long did you think it would take me to realise?'

Kulp wished he had that sort of ability. 'Tricked you? Why should I trick you?'

'Dax and Reniola knew I was coming. They duped me into believing I had devoured them.'

Kulp detected the tone of paranoia. Until then, the Olmuke had been so full of his own self importance he had assumed the entity's megalomania to be quite normal. In a different galaxy, the flaw was alarmingly apparent.

'I never told Dax and Reniola anything. I want them dead as much as you do,' Kulp lied, wishing just one of them would materialise and hold his clammy hand. 'You trapped them in that valley and wiped them out.'

'They were energy illusions. I did not know this until I had swallowed them.'

'Don't blame me because they gave you indigestion.'

A bolt of lightning struck the ground and scorched Kulp's boots.

'You will lead me to them this time or...'

Kulp didn't need to be told. Being devoured was the only other option. Not wanting to be transformed into a mouthful of green goo, he told Krykal, 'All right.

Just turn down the lightning so I can come out of
cover.'

There was a dangerously long pause. Eventually
the electrical storm retreated to the sky and Kulp
tumbled from his makeshift bunker of roots and
bracken. He had no intention of staying in the open for
long. Keeping low, just in case Krykal thought it might
pick him off for target practise, Kulp stumbled down
an incline to see if he could find a much deeper shelter.
All the caves he checked out had the frightened eyes of
the planet's wildlife staring back at him. Even wolves
and deer had decided on a truce for the sake of some
decent cover.

Kulp was unsure what to do next. His blaster was
puny against an entity made of pure energy; Krykal
would have absorbed its power like a bonfire collecting
the fizz of a sparkler. Then, at last, sensible thought
began to seep back into his mind. Of course - it was an
energy problem! Simple maths - he could solve that.
All those lightning strikes Krykal had been making
into Moosevan's planet must have increased her mass.

Before he could fathom a way to work on the idea,
a glittering shape blocked his path.

He halted, dazzled and daunted. 'Dax?'

'Dax,' grated the humourless reply.

If Kulp had said how glad he was to see her, she
wouldn't have believed him. 'How's Reniola?' he tried
to humour instead.

'Very cramped for an entity who likes a lot of skin
to exist in.' The voice sounded as though it was
crunching diamonds.

'I didn't really mean to try and annihilate either of
you.'

'Well, give us fair warning when you do mean it
because you nearly succeeded.'

Kulp suddenly left the ground and found he was
suspended a bone-breaking distance from it. 'Now,

don't be hasty Dax, You know you aren't supposed to
kill anyone.'

'Oh, I've something better than that in mind.'

On second thoughts, death sounded better.

'What are you going to do, Dax? I can't use the
portal, my spacesuit's torn.' Desperation overwhelmed
him. 'Look, I can help you overcome Krykal. I won't
double cross you! I swear!'

Kulp could have sworn until the sky turned purple.
He felt himself suddenly spinning then, like a fly
suspended in amber, all sensation stopped. He looked
about him.

He didn't like what he saw.

CHAPTER 35

Albright and Diana returned to the cave only to find
the others gone. The Colonel started to load his
revolver. This time Diana didn't try to dissuade him.
Moosevan was too occupied to do anything about it and
didn't need to be distracted by the machinations of
annoying humans.

Not knowing where his strength came from,
Albright made it to the top of the hill facing the cave.
The lightning had died down, though the air still
crackled with a dull charge.

The other three were nowhere to be seen. Any one
of them could have engineered a catastrophe by
themselves but, with the other two to stop them, it
could only mean that something terrible had
happened.

Albright put a reassuring arm about Diana's
shoulders. 'They can't have gone far. They probably
went out to collect some water when the lightning
stopped.'

'What? All three of them, and they don't have so
much as a polystyrene cup between them.'

At that, Albright felt the weight of their predicament bear down and, just in case one of them burst into tears, he pulled a handkerchief from his pocket. Reniola's small box tumbled out with it.

On hitting the ground, it began to leap about like a demented grasshopper.

Diana looked at it blankly. 'It must be filled with jumping beans.'

'Pretty exotic ones, given the height they're jumping.'

The box became even more gymnastic and they both moved back to watch apprehensively. After leaping into the air and spinning rapidly, it shattered. In a cloud of dust, curses, and spluttering, Reniola landed before them like a huge, suddenly released, mattress of fur. She was very dishevelled and not in the best of moods. Albright now realised who had saved his life, probably at the risk of being devoured by Krykal. Unable to stop himself, he threw his arms about the surprised entity.

Reniola gave a self conscious, whiskery grin. 'Sorry about the operation. Would have made a neater job of it, but daren't stay materialised for any longer. How are you, old thing?'

'Julia and the others are missing.'

'Oh, probably out for a stroll.'

Diana wasn't so conciliatory. However dismissively she may have treated her own daughter, she resented an alien seeming so off-hand about the girl being in danger. 'They've more than likely been cornered by your dratted dinosaurs, and the Colonel wouldn't have been injured if you hadn't brought him here in the first place,' she scolded.

Reniola didn't say anything because the dinosaurs were a more plausible explanation. She shook out her crumpled fur like a sodden old English sheep dog and straightened her tail. 'All right then. Stay here. Won't be long.'

Without warning, she disappeared.

Diana put her arms about Albright. 'Hey, I'm the one who's meant to be snivelling, remember.'

'I'm sorry. I'm not used to all these frights, you know. Soldiers are trained to believe they're the ones putting the fear of Hades into everyone else.'

'How many would sign up if the army advertised for cannon fodder?'

'As long as they can wear a uniform, some men are idiot enough to apply for anything.'

'Julia could explain that. She studies something called Social Engineering at school.'

'What on earth for?'

'Probably so the pupils don't grow up like us.'

Albright, still shaky, folded his handkerchief and tucked it back in his pocket. 'It's not always a good thing to have a child who understands you. You can't get away with anything, y' know.'

'Your daughter sounds a fearsome lady?'

'No, she's very sweet, really, considering she's spent all her life in a wheelchair.'

Diana wasn't sure whether she ought to ask why. 'Oh?'

'Angela's mother had an accident when she was carrying her. She died, but they managed to save the baby. Angela's brain wasn't damaged, thank God; she studied and became a maths tutor.' Albright shrugged. 'All beyond me, of course. She took after her maternal grandfather. He proved some wonderful theory I can't remember the name of.'

'The fundamentalists aren't giving her a rough time, are they?' Diana asked carefully.

'Goodness no, they wouldn't understand a word she published. Anyway, just in case, Angela has worked out an equation to prove the existence of virtually any god.'

'Will she believe what happened to you?'

'She might even be able to think out a proof for that as well.'

'Let me know if she succeeds so I can believe it as well.'

Albright sighed, 'If I survive this, I think I'll retire. Do some gardening for Angela. She likes her garden.'

'Only have room for snails and washing in mine. Don't need a large garden. We've got the meadow to look out at.'

'I wonder if there are any worms on Titan?' Albright suddenly mused.

'Must be a few slugs. Something's still eating the fuchsias.'

Albright at last smiled. 'Wouldn't that be some sort of justice. The only other species human beings have to share their planet with; a few slugs and worms to eat their mortal remains.'

'I wonder how much they depend on oxygen.'

CHAPTER 36

Yuri, Salisbury, and Julia cowered as close to the rock face as they could, but the dinosaurs surrounding them had their own winkle pickers. Having seen what one of them did to Albright, panic began to set in. Despite curses, threats, and pleading from the other two, Yuri was unable to rouse Moosevan and he irrationally scrabbled about the wall as though he could open a crevice to pack them into.

The deinonychids closed in. The two men pushed Julia behind them and shut their eyes. They heard the scratching of massive-sickle clawed feet as they came close and closer and felt the stench of breath putrid with the remains of their last meal.

'I am sorry, Salisbury,' Yuri suddenly blurted out.

'Why, old man?'

'I have been mean to you, but I like you really.'

Salisbury uncharitably thought he might have made this revelation when there had been more time to appreciate it. Nevertheless, out of courtesy, he decided to concede, 'I suppose I must have seemed quite a pain to you, but that's the way I'm made. Never was one to make friends easily.'

'We are friends now?'

Salisbury wound his long arms about Julia and Yuri. 'Yes, of course.'

Without warning the scratching of claws stopped. It was replaced by the jingling of ornaments dangling from a rather natty waistcoat.

'I say you three, I wish you would stop tormenting the wildlife. This is a conservation zone, you know.'

They opened their eyes. A familiar, plump creature with a swishing tail was standing over several comatose dinosaurs. It had never occurred to any of them they would actually be glad to see Reniola, though Yuri wondered if a terrible death was preferable after making his confession to Salisbury.

'Where's Mum and the Colonel?' demanded Julia.

'They're all right.'

'They disappeared from the cave. Where did they go?'

Reniola was baffled for a moment. She had the feeling that this was something she should know about. Diana had never been as easy to read as Yuri and Salisbury. It didn't help that the woman had an open manner which persuaded others she wasn't capable of plotting anything. From experience, Reniola knew better.

'Disappeared, did they?' the entity enquired diffidently.

'We thought they had been trapped by...' Salisbury indicated that the slumbering sickle claws. 'Those things.'

'What? Diana?' Reniola smiled. 'She's not that daft.'

Salisbury flushed in annoyance, although it was difficult to deny.

'The Colonel couldn't have gone that far anyway,' scoffed Julia. 'It wasn't my idea to come out and look for them, you know. I really thought it was a pretty silly thing to do.'

Salisbury wondered who had been responsible for educating this precocious child. Julia wasn't taking their predicament as seriously as she should. She might at least try to panic more convincingly.

Yuri sat on the ground and burst into tears.

Reniola looked puzzled, and Salisbury embarrassed.

Julia wrapped her arms about him.

'What's the matter, Yuri?'

He mopped away the tears with his sleeve. 'They have ruined astronomy.' He pointed to Reniola. 'That fuzzy creature and glittery friend... Nothing will ever be the same. Centuries it took to map heavens and they... they rearrange everything into wrong place. There should be law to stop them.'

'Now don't go and have a tantrum, Yuri. You'll only give yourself a headache - and Reniola did save our lives after all. We should really feel privileged to be at the centre of all this.'

Yuri didn't like the Adrian Mole tone in her voice. 'You feel privileged if you want. You young not have sense to know when they have been exploited.'

Reniola backed away uneasily. 'Oh well, better go now. Old lightning still wants to devour me, you know.'

'We thought it had.'

'Me? Goodness no. I'm not that stupid, you know.'

CHAPTER 37

As Kulp floated about the inside of a huge bubble with an impenetrable, clear shell, he tried to make sense of where he was. Legend had it that a place like this existed somewhere in the grimy mists of time, but there was no logic in anyone wanting to gather together specimens from every life form in Kulp's old, rundown galaxy. What would have been the point? The only logical reason must have been that it was because the galaxy was running down, and some intellectual beings with an obsession for catalogues were collecting specimens of everything from plankton to supernovae before they became extinct. The Olmuke qualified more than most; they had abolished females and had no choice but to produce their young from a deteriorating stock of eggs.

Kulp now discovered that he was a mere worm slammed between the pages of a mouldering book it should have been eating. The guards in this place could not be bribed because they had no need of mortal pleasures. Like Dax and Reniola, they were pure energy, and probably distant relations. All the serious aggravation in Kulp's criminal career had been generated by entities of pure energy. Why couldn't they have been more manageable, like the grotesque Mott or their equally megalomaniacal androids? Even though they had very nearly knocked the grey stuffing out of him, at least he could understand them. Now, he faced an eternity with puffs of energy that were too evolved to empathise with mortal biologies and, when he died, could well pickle his body for research. And whatever had become of Tolt and Jannu, his former partners in crime? Why hadn't they been selected to join him? Perhaps not Tolt: as the Olmuke egg stocks

deteriorated, his intellect had been an omen of things
to come.

Kulp would have screamed and scratched the
energy shield if he could move or make a sound. Like
all the other inert specimens about him, he would soon
learn to just watch and live in his thoughts.

CHAPTER 38

Lightning once more rained down on Earth. Reniola
wasn't sure whether Krykal was after her and Dax, or
the planet dweller inside it. To ensure Yuri, Salisbury,
and Julia were not caught upwind of more predators,
she conjured up sliding doors to the overhang they
sheltered beneath.

Diana watched from her hillside vantage point
with a manic satisfaction that quite unsettled Albright.
As she was now so accustomed to dealing with aliens,
he suspected something otherworldly had rubbed off on
her. This was no middle-aged housewife resigned to
terminal boredom. This woman was intense, electric,
and slightly mad. In his own way, Albright understood.
If he managed to return to humdrum existence, he
would never be able to change back into an eccentric
blip on the notice board of normality. The only thing
that now bothered him was the secret Diana and the
planet dweller shared. He wanted her to take cover,
yet daren't insist. It would have been like telling a
duck to stay out of the rain.

'I have feeling we are all going to die again,' Yuri
muttered unhappily as he crouched on the floor.

'You mean, you again have the feeling that we all
are going to die,' corrected Salisbury.

Yuri looked contemptuously at the orange and
purple striped shirt Reniola had given Salisbury
because his other had been shredded into bandages to
bind Albright's wounds. The contrast with the

brownish grey waistcoat projected the colours all the more jarringly. Having admitted in a moment of uncontrolled terror that he had been unreasonable towards the don, it was a little premature to start telling him to go to Hell. The Russian pulled up his knees, buried his face in them and longed for a bottle of gin. Moosevan was too occupied to supply some herbal substitute, and Reniola was watching at the small cave's sliding doors in case Krykal sensed her presence and sent a few deadly shafts in their direction. Now things were no longer going to plan, the lightning entity seemed more interested in attacking the planet.

'When I get back home I'm going to do a paper round and save up for a DVD recorder,' Julia announced suddenly.

'Oh, the optimism of youth,' groaned Yuri.

'Why shouldn't I get a paper round? Old Mrs Squire's kids never stay long.'

'I meant, you seem sure we get back home.'

'Oh don't be so depressing Yuri. What is the matter with you?'

Yuri shook his tangled grey locks. 'I have been put on world that should really orbit Saturn, kidnapped by idiot entity, and brought to Earth where I am nearly burnt to crisp by lightning, and eaten by dinosaurs, and have been stuck with company of teacher who thinks pronouncing something wrong is worse than having it happen to you... That is what is wrong with me! '

Julia put her arms about his shoulders. 'Yuri... Why don't you say something nice to Mr Salisbury? I know you like him really. You said so.'

'I thought I was about to die.'

'He doesn't have to if he's not keen on the idea,' Salisbury said testily.

'You're both behaving like children.' Something

then occurred to Julia; her mind wasn't quite as immature as they thought. 'You're both jealous of Colonel Albright, aren't you?'

The ensuing silence was more charged than the lightning-riven sky outside.

Julia giggled. 'Oh dear... I wonder why Mum has that effect on men?'

She's too independent for her own good,' Salisbury said huffily.

'I hope you grow up into hippopotamus with bleached hair,' Yuri told her.

'Who can't take the truth then.'

'I must admit I prefer you watching the television,' agreed Salisbury.

'When I grow up I am going to be an airline pilot and have a steward in every airport.'

'If you grow up...'

CHAPTER 39

Dax cast a web about the stratosphere, a luminous lattice of pure energy woven with warps of the planet's natural gravity to contain Krykal long enough for her to manoeuvre the entity back through Kulp's gravity portal. She was unaware that Diana and Moosevan had other ideas about dealing with the rapacious creature.

***

Albright gave up hinting that Diana should take cover and decided to join her in a game of Russian roulette even Yuri wasn't crazy enough to play, and watched her silently talking to the planet with her thoughts. It was now apparent that what he had seen in the cave was part of a scheme her and Moosevan had thought up. Diana's solution to Krykal was too simple for intelligences as advanced as Dax and Reniola to work out, and Albright only realised how dangerous it was when a shaft of plasma roared up through the ground, singeing his uniform braid. The energy pierced the atmosphere filled with Krykal's lightning, sparkling like a gigantic Roman candle. The lightning entity revolved wildly, attracted to something it didn't have the mass to resist. Kyrkal stopped bombarding the landscape and focussed its attack on the incandescent anomaly.

Diana concentrated and was able to see through Moosevan's mind. From a mortal perspective it looked as though they were winning.

The grass about them turned into hay in the heat, but Diana was too occupied to notice the ends of her hair frizzle, or plastic buckles on her shoes start to melt.

'This is it,' Albright muttered to himself. For all his efforts in resisting engagement with the enemy, it looked as though it was his destiny to end up as a scorch mark on the blistered ground. The only comfort was in knowing it would be quick, like standing directly under ground zero. It was just as well his daughter would never know what had happened to him. She would have had some heroic verse or other carved on his tombstone.

Just as he was resigned to his fate, there was a blinding light like a thousand dawns... then blackness.

After that, Albright wasn't sure whether he had the right to be alive. There were too many aches and pains and a persistent ringing in his ears for it to be Heaven. If Gabriel played a trumpet like that, he would never have got into the Musicians' Union, celestial or otherwise. As his retinas recovered, the Colonel was aware that Krykal's lightning and Moosevan's pillar of energy had vanished and, to his amazement, Diana had escaped without as much as a blister. She must have lied about being only an

unmarried mother and was really the manifestation of
some asbestos deity after all.

Albright's throat was unbearably dry. 'What
happened?' he croaked. 'Where did the lightning go?'

'To Earth.'

'To Earth?'

'Moosevan swallowed it.'

'But...' Albright pulled himself up. 'That lightning
creature was meant to devour her?'

'So... the best laid plans of idiot entities and
Olmuke engineers...'

'But... how?'

'Moosevan and Krykal were both energy. The
lightning entity just hadn't counted on the planet
dweller having more of it.'

'You mean... she ate it?'

Diana shrugged. 'Something like that.'

'How is she going to digest the thing? It must have
doubled her mass.'

'Oh yes.'

Albright realised that her artless manner
concealed a capacity for intrigue a Borgia would have
envied and looked at her sternly. 'This was your idea,
wasn't it?'

Diana shrugged again in innocent non-committal.

'So what happens now?' he asked.

'A large increase in mass for a creature like a
planet dweller can only mean one thing.'

'Only one?'

'Or perhaps two, three, or four, or more...'

Albright became as white as rice paper. 'She
can't... She's not like us.'

'Yuri could explain it. The mathematics of mass is
beyond me. I even have problems weighing out flour
for a cake.'

'Just as well most ingredients no longer exist.'

Diana smiled calculatingly. 'I knew you wouldn't

let it bother you.'

'I feel sick.'

***

As Yuri and Salisbury occasionally scowled at Julia, who they mutually had to admit was becoming a pain in the neck, there was a jolt as though something had kicked the floor.

Yuri gingerly put his ear to the ground: he didn't like what he detected.

'Well?' asked Salisbury.

'Oh dear,' said Yuri. 'Oh dear.' Then he turned quite wan.

'What is it, then?' Reniola demanded from the entrance, still trying to work out where Krykal had gone.

'This I do not like to say.' Yuri resumed his position on the floor and buried his face in his knees.

***

Having waited for what it considered to be long enough, the Dringle tossed caution to the searing solar wind and started to press buttons. Inside the space ship this was all right because it understood the basic controls, but then it transferred its interest to the portal...

CHAPTER 40

In resignation, Dax rolled up the web she had spread across the planet's stratosphere to ensnare Krykal. Diana and Moosevan had thrown everything out of kilter, not to mention destroying the entity she gone to such pains to evict from the solar system. There was nothing Dax could do now apart from dash off and ensure all the results had their own ecosystems.

Why she had ever allowed herself to become involved with human beings, a dead end species cluttering up a planet that had the potential to produce a more promising life form? Perhaps if dolphins hadn't exchanged paws for flippers and given up legs... But then, where was the point in thinking about it now? Wherever she stuck them, Dax was still responsible for the welfare of the human race, complete with its self importance, pollution, massacres, and other annoying little habits. Where to put them this time, though? Nothing had gone to plan thanks to Kulp and Diana, and the solar system would soon be a very crowded place. It was just as well Reniola had been uncharacteristically useful and sent a huge moon from the Earth's distant past.

CHAPTER 41

'At long last!' whooped Eva as though she had discovered Planet X, little suspecting that some interfering entity was already manoeuvring it out of its orbit to where it would become a commonplace body in astronomers' lenses.

'What is it?' asked Honey, at last giving up on a few moments sleep; Eva was the noisiest astronomer she had ever worked with.

'Everything's started to line up.'

'You mean, they're falling back into their centre of gravity?'

'No...' Eva said. 'They appear to be lining up.'

'Let me see.' Honey tossed her blanket aside and padded over in her stockinged feet. She looked into the eyepiece. 'How can you tell?'

'I've been watching them for three hours.'

'You should have a permanent squint.'

'Well, get your Captain friend to order the power company to turn on the main circuits so we can use the computer.'

Honey came across something more interesting. 'Hold on.'

'What?'

'Mars is leaving its orbit.'

'Don't be ridiculous.' Eva rummaged amongst her notes, then realised that Honey was right. The Red Planet shouldn't be in the frame. 'Where's it going?'

'Difficult to tell, but it's definitely been diverted from its orbit.'

Eva elbowed her aside. 'I think you're right.'

'I wonder what Venus is doing?'

Eva gave Honey a stony glare. 'It won't be up for another hour. Why don't we check on Jupiter and Saturn while we're at it?'

'I don't think the gas giants are any good to whoever's shifting things about. There must be some Galactic authority we can complain to.'

'Would take several hundred years in the post. It might be as well to stick with the lunatics doing the interfering. However inconsistent, they might get their act together in the end.'

'I'd rather they got it together before the end.'

CHAPTER 42

Kulp fell into a semi aware stupor as he became acclimatised to his confinement. Suddenly something slammed him against the wall of his bubble as though trying to drag him through it. In his terror, he found he could move just enough to fasten his spacesuit, which Dax had obligingly mended to send him through the gravity portal. The keepers of the endangered species in their zoo were either unaware of what was happening, busy stocktaking somewhere else, or they may have thought this sudden burst of energy was the new specimen's way of venting frustration.

There was nothing Kulp could hang on to and the jerking about continued until he felt like meringue mix, well beaten and very stiff. One final jerk

catapulted his atoms into another dimension. He was
no longer spinning in a tumble drier, but being
snapped backwards and forwards like a jet propelled
yoyo. By the time they struck something solid, he
wasn't conscious enough to realise that the Dringle
had been meddling with Dax's programming to the
portal and, yet again, was responsible for releasing
him from prison.

The Olmuke's molecules, although in a form that
resembled Kulp, were spinning too fast for their owner
to communicate whether he appreciated the Dringle's
interference or wanted to hang it with its own tail. The
Dringle wasn't quite sure what to make of Kulp's
return either. It hadn't intended to rescue him, and
couldn't comprehend why the green engineer should
have been that put out. At least it raised the Dringle's
hopes of getting the money the arch criminal owed it.

CHAPTER 43

Salisbury took a deep lungful of the sweet air at long
last free of electrostatic charge. He felt positively
content, despite the purple and orange shirt Reniola
had inflicted on him. The subdued Yuri crouched in his
corner, shaking his head as though trying to fight off
vertigo.

There was another blow from inside the planet,
but they had got used to them, except Yuri because he
knew what was causing it.

Do we have to go back home now?' Julia asked,
trying not to sound too dejected. Aware the other two
hadn't enjoyed the experience at all, she didn't want to
start another argument.

Reniola was trying to straighten her whiskers
after the electrical storm had curled them into an
absurd moustache. 'Dax might take a little longer than
we calculated. No one expected Kulp to turn up and

interfere.'

'Where is Kulp?'

Reniola shrugged. 'No idea. I'd be careful where
you walk, though, and avoid any smouldering green
puddles.'

'Ugh!'

'Olmukes are very oily when rendered down by
heat, you know.'

'Do you mind?' asked Salisbury. 'I may not feel
that hungry, but there's no need to permanently kill
my appetite for anything green. That will now be the
principal colour of our food thanks to your interfering.
Not unless Moosevan can come up with something
more palatable, of course.'

'Moosevan, she is too busy to make us food...'
muttered Yuri.

'What's he on about?' asked Julia.

Salisbury hadn't a clue. 'Probably withdrawal
symptoms from something or other.'

'You laugh now.' Yuri sounded rather Rasputinish
and the others withdrew a little at his sinister tone.
'But you will see...'

'Oh well,' Reniola decided, 'Suppose I'd better leave
you lot with some shelter and food now the dinos have
gone. Can't stop any longer.'

'Where's mum, then?'

Reniola waved a furry finger and the cave's sliding
doors disappeared. She indicated two figures in the
distance. 'Now, you will all behave yourselves, won't
you? We have to alter our plans, and that's going to be
very tricky.'

'Trickier than you think, super intelligence,'
chuckled Yuri quietly.

Reniola half ignored him. Like a sorcerer casting a
spell, she pointed to a meadow above them and
conjured up a rather splendid chalet with a banquet
inside. 'Plenty of stuff in the fridge as well. Taps might

be a bit stiff, though. Could never get the hang of plumbing.'

'If you're able to do that,' pondered Julia, 'why can't you straighten your whiskers or understand what Yuri's going on about?'

Reniola didn't bother to answer. It was easier to disappear.

As soon as she had gone, Julia dashed from the cave and up to the chalet, expecting to find a television.

Salisbury and Yuri rushed over to Albright and Diana.

'We thought you might have been in trouble of some sort,' gushed Salisbury.

'We look for you,' protested Yuri. 'But dinosaurs find us first,' he added with an edge of doom and disapproval in his voice.

'I'm glad you're all right,' Diana said. 'What's the matter with Yuri?'

Yuri's tone became more manic. 'You ask what is matter with me? You tell Moosevan to do this, don't you? It is all your fault.'

Salisbury sighed. 'What is he on about?'

Albright smiled mysteriously. 'He's going to be a daddy.'

Salisbury gave Diana a look of stunned betrayal.

'Not me you fool!' She snapped. 'I'm well past that.'

'Who then?'

Diana and Albright looked at each other. It seemed heartless to kick him in his naiveté, but it was better than Yuri doing it whilst in the depths of this malevolent mood.

'It's a sort of... replication,' Diana tried to explain. 'More a matter of matter... If you see what I mean.' It was obvious Salisbury didn't. 'Different species reproduce in different ways.'

'I have children,' he announced rather stiffly as

though she were attacking the possibility. 'I've also kept a dog and rather randy cat - I do know a little about procreation.'

'Well, we're not talking about that kind.'

Yuri frowned as though just realising he had been nursing a crush on a cosmic absurdity. He wasn't sure whether he was going to forgive himself for it. 'They mean that this is more to do with mass and mathematics.'

Diana shrugged. 'I have trouble working out when I've been short-changed in the supermarket, but that sounds about right.'

'What is going on?' insisted Salisbury.

Yuri gave him a pitying look. 'When mass increases, it can do many things. It may have nuclear reaction and switch on like sun ...'

Salisbury gasped in alarm. 'Oh... She wouldn't dare?'

'Moosevan can not keep that much mass... Or she would implode and make gravitational field which would shrink Earth.'

'Oh, my goodness...'

'But Moosevan is entity of strange whims. She may not remember how planet dwellers like her came to exist.' Yuri gave Diana a penetrating glare. 'But someone remind her.' Salisbury shook his head. 'I'm still not very clear about what you mean?'

Yuri shrugged, and then shared glances with Diana and Albright, who gave up and left to join Julia in the chalet.

CHAPTER 44

'Now this is really interesting...' said Eva. She turned from the reflector's eyepiece to the Captain. 'Surely someone in NASA is observing this, for goodness sake?'

But that was not in the Captain's brief. 'They had to close down. The Movement for Planetary Non-Interference fire bombed their observatories.'

'The what?'

'They're a breakaway group of the Goddess Earth Society. They don't particularly want to be at the centre of the Universe, just prefer to ignore anything with an orbit that suggests we aren't.'

Eva was too much of a cynic to disbelieve her. 'And they managed to work out what an orbit was in only a few weeks?' She returned to her observations.

'The human race has been sickening for an outbreak of universal fundamentalism for years. This is just the rash. Wait until the fever breaks out.'

Eva grunted. 'Venus's cloud cover seems to be breaking up. Just as well nothing was living on it.'

***

Unbeknown to the astronomers, there was a rather eccentric species inhabiting the corrosive, crushing environment of Venus. The Volcanic Zatts were extremely bad-tempered and tended to attack anything which survived their atmosphere for more than what seemed a decent length of time. They suspected the change in their planet had something to do with the strange entity they had caught surveying it a short while ago. Nothing could be done about her, so they retreated to their volcanoes and wondered how well they would manage to survive if their planet became temperate: perhaps they wouldn't need to be so bad-tempered.

Buried deep beneath the dusty surface of Mars were the ruins of an ancient civilisation. As a protected planet it should have been left in its long, undisturbed sleep. Now something seemed intent on waking it up. The ice caps of carbon dioxide started to melt and flow, its thin atmosphere thickened, and the mantle began

to rumble with plate movement. The larger moons of
the gaseous planets, which had not already been
stolen, whirled from their orbits. Like a procession of
cosmic bridesmaids, they danced towards an orbit
nearer the sun.

Soon, there was an evenly spaced ring of planets,
moons, and asteroids sharing the Earth and Titan's
orbit.

CHAPTER 45

Diana and the others sat and waited inside their
chalet. Whatever his scholarly achievements, Salisbury
had never been strong on imagination, and he
preferred not to work out what was about to happen
anyway.

Diana should have felt guilty about putting the
idea into Moosevan's mind. Human families were
monstrous enough, and she was unsure whether it had
been a good idea to share her inconsistent mothering
instincts with the planet dweller.

Outside, the sky darkened to an unusual magenta
and heavenly curtains of orange - similar to the colour
in Salisbury's shirt - rippled about it like an aurora.
The bright rim of the horizon seemed to quiver and
those animals that had only just plucked up the
courage to leave their caves and forage dashed for
cover. Where was the point in a world without humans
when the elements wouldn't behave reasonably?

Great stretches of the Earth's crust shimmered
and took on concave shapes. All the zebras, bison,
camels, and wildebeest had the sense to stampede
away from the monstrous blisters, and those
developing below the oceans were given wide berths by
whales and barracuda.

The dark pink clouds above the chalet started to
churn like wool being carded on the serrated sides of

mountains. Then they abruptly disappeared to leave
the sky a colour no sane milliner would contemplate,
feathered with a golden orange that would have looked
more convincing on an erupting volcano.

Julia, having discovered a television, but nowhere
to plug it in, dashed outside to watch. Diana swallowed
her biscuit and followed.

'This is not good,' Yuri muttered, glowering at the
remains of the large meal as though it had been
drugged.

'What's wrong, old boy?' asked Albright.

'They have rearranged solar system in less time it
would take to travel from London to Paris.'

'But what for?' demanded Salisbury.

'Probably like the urge humans have to shift the
furniture about every now and then,' evaded Albright.

Salisbury petulantly crumpled his napkin and
tossed it onto the table before going outside to join
Julia and Diana.

'I do not think that man is really happy as human
being,' Yuri commented.

Albright nodded. He was beginning to wonder if
life would be less hassle if he were a pot plant.

A pair of eyes too large for their body gazed at
them from the French windows. A small muntjac
entered and snuffled about the furnishings, then
nipped at the tablecloth in the hope of something sweet
falling to the floor. Albright gathered a handful of cake
icing. The deer crunched up the offering then
wandered back out.

'What a difference lack of humans are having on
the wildlife,' the soldier observed.

'There is probably wolf waiting behind sundial to
eat it.'

'Julia is right, you know...'

'Why is she right?'

'You are becoming melancholic. Why not just

accept what is happening and look upon it as a happy occasion?'

'So where will Dax and Reniola put human race this time?'

'They've probably refitted a cosy nook somewhere. Might even let us back here.'

Yuri grunted. He knew that planet dwellers preferred homes to themselves. On her original planet Moosevan ruled supreme and juggled the landscape as the whim took her. Here, she had to be careful for fear of injuring the creatures. It was unlikely that preference would change however many there were.

At last Julia was engrossed by something that wasn't happening on a television screen. 'I always wondered where baby planets came from, Mum. If my science teacher can see this, I bet he won't believe anything the text books say ever again.'

Diana mused on how scruffy her daughter's school uniform was, even before she had grown out of it, and could see that she would have to lash out on another one well before she became a fully developed, busty adolescent. 'Fancy Moosevan waiting until this time in life to divide into a family,' she unwisely mused.

'Well, you put the thought into her mind. They're not going to let you forget that, you know.'

Salisbury joined then. 'What thought into whose head?'

Diana sighed and reluctantly admitted, 'Moosevan is replicating.'

Salisbury was silent for a moment. He was well aware what "replicating" meant, yet could not immediately apply it to Moosevan. It was difficult to visualize something which couldn't be seen, then multiply it. Perhaps Diana meant "reproducing". He shuddered at the thought, even though it made better sense. 'You mean..?'

'That's right. Swallowing the lightning entity gave

her so much mass she has to divide into lots of little planet dwellers.'

'Oh goodness. I'd never have guessed.'

'We gathered that.'

'Is that why Yuri is so put out?'

'He feels responsible.'

'How ludicrous.' Salisbury was nevertheless relieved that the progeny were arriving while he was not the lover in favour. Then something occurred to him. Others were usually more careless with the English language than he was, so he decided Diana didn't really mean "replicating".

'You mean, she's dividing... Like cells?'

Diana nodded. 'Like bloody big cells. So there won't be any more Moosevan to try and light your fire.'

Even though he knew his timber had always been too damp anyway, Salisbury still needed reassuring. 'Are you positive?'

'They'll all be far too young for romance'

The sky continued to grow darken, so everyone decided to get some sleep. Just in case there were any of Reniola's dinosaurs still wandering the countryside, Albright made sure nothing could get a talon under a window latch. Yuri slumped in a corner and wondered why, considering all the other miracles taking place, some benevolent entity couldn't supply some gin to anaesthetize his senses, and Julia at last managed to get a picture, albeit quite baffling, out of the television. Diana, not too sure where the signal was coming from, confiscated the remote control and sent her to bed.

CHAPTER 46

As the sun came up, the power was restored to Eva's main observatory and, at last, other telescopes about the planet were provided with enough security to operate. From all corners of the planet strange reports

started to flow in. The Earth and Titan were no longer
the only ones sharing the same orbit. For as far as
satellites could track, a string of worlds appeared to be
circling the sun like a necklace of irregular sized
pearls. Each had its own weather system and
atmosphere, and looked a darn sight more stable than
the ecosystem on Titan. Now perhaps, assuming the
bumbling alien intelligences had got their act together,
all the businessmen, bankers, estate agents, and local
government officers could have one planet, all the
conservationists and vegetarians another, and so on...
Eva had the feeling they were already booked,
however.

***

To achieve this feat of planetary engineering, Dax and
Reniola had called on help. Their own cosmic species
were dimensions away and too consumed with solving
Universal problems to be immediately bothered about
what their two agents were doing in some galactic
backwater. They wondered why they had sent them in
the first place to clean up the galaxy Kulp came from,
only to have them ploughing up the weeds in someone
else's garden. It was a bit too late to remind them of
their commitment to non interference. They gave Dax
and Reniola the powers they needed and hoped that
would be the last they heard from them.

CHAPTER 47

When Diana woke, the sky still had a magenta hue to
it and, as the sun came up, it turned pale rose pink,
then salmon, until an orange shell surrounded the
Earth. She roused the others, apart from Yuri who was
already outside scowling at the sky.
        'What's that golden glow over there, Mum?' Julia
pointed to a huge sphere of light rising above the

160

horizon like a fuzzy sun. It wriggled a little like some cosmic tadpole. Once free from the planet's rim it started to spin then, like a comet escaping the Earth's atmosphere, soared off into space.

'Was that a baby planet dweller, Mum?'

Yuri's scowl deepened, so Diana thought twice about attempting an answer.

'This is only energy mass,' snapped Yuri. 'It is dividing. It is not like real birth.'

'Then what will happen to Moosevan?'

'She will be no more.'

Julia had never learnt anything like this in biology classes and it had little to do with any physics she could comprehend. The schoolgirl only just understood what made rainbows and why tin cans crumpled when the air was pumped out of them.

She sighed. 'Oh... Poor Moosevan.'

Yuri gave her a suspicious glance as though she had been communicating with the planet dweller as well, then realised that it was only an adolescent affectation.

He grunted. 'Now there will be many Moosevans.'

Albright gave a chuckle. 'Think of all the rows they'll be in the UN about what names to give them.'

'I've a feeling they're going to be big enough to name themselves,' Diana said.

'There's another one over there, and another.'

About a dozen golden spheres left the planet's surface. Diana assumed they were travelling to the string of sparkling planets they had seen against the purple sky the night before.

Eventually the Earth's moon, which had been taking a back seat during all the excitement, started to glow in the daylight sky as it was fleshed with an atmosphere and seas.

'It's not as big as that moon we saw on the dinosaur's planet is it, Mum?'

Diana felt uneasy as she wondered who this moon was being dressed up for and what had happened to the one Reniola had abducted.

Before she could voice her misgivings, the chalet behind them vanished as a familiar mist engulfed the party.

'Oh shit!' snapped Diana. 'Reniola's timing is worse than a one-legged flamenco dancer's.'

She could have sworn all she liked, but it wouldn't have stopped anyone from being dumped back into the bizarre reality of polluted tap water, laddered tights and children who craved DVD recorders. Reniola must have believed human beings couldn't survive if separated from the humdrum for too long.

Salisbury was dropped into the seat of his car, much to his and a traffic warden's surprise; Yuri fell onto the overgrown lawn of his front garden, and Albright almost landed in the arms of the Captain who had been sent to find him. Diana found herself in her living room and Julia in front of the television set. Most of the abducted dinosaurs ended up in a totally different solar system on a planet where the plants were able to run about and lasso lunch with their tendrils. This was quite a novel experience for the sickle claws. Their descendants became aquatic and molested nothing more substantial than plankton: when confronted by carnivorous conifers, even a tyrannosaur's appetite loses its edge.

Diana aimed a frustrated kick at the tea trolley, which catapulted into the settee and scattered its bowl of fruit over the cushions. She took a deep breath, then another. The air seemed quite fresh. This couldn't be the real Earth... could it? The nearest person who might have answered that with any certainty would be totally blotto by the time the stars came out and incapable of knowing where he was, let alone what planet he was on.

Diana went into the kitchen and switched on the kettle.

There was a sudden commotion in the buddleia outside. She hadn't heard its like for so long she jumped. Two starlings were squabbling. Not daring to believe her eyes, she cautiously went out into the small garden. Somewhere in the distance a dog barked and cat skirled. The sounds were hardly musical but, at that moment, they sounded sweeter than Mario Lanza.

This had to be Earth.

CHAPTER 48

Having reassured the surprised Captain that he wasn't going to make a habit of appearing out of nowhere, Colonel Albright straightened his uniform and demanded to know what was going on.

She locked the Land Rover and pointed to Eva's observatory. 'Just going to see if the space telescope has faxed anything to the Doctor yet. Honey Paymaster is with her. They've been sleeping in the observatory.' She hesitated as though about to ask some intimate detail of his personal life. 'Excuse me asking, Sir, but what did happen to you?'

'Anyone asked for a report yet?'

'Not yet. Must be too busy.'

'Then you wouldn't like to forget that I disappeared, would you?'

The Captain looked at the Colonel as though he was an optical illusion. He smiled genially and she became even more suspicious. 'What about the others who disappeared at the same time?'

'Probably all emanations of my fevered imagination. I'm going to apply for retirement anyway. Might mean a promotion for you.'

She didn't look too elated about that prospect. The Captain had considered giving up her uniform to become a night club hostess when the planets first started to have hysterics. Being over six feet tall, she knew she was bound to fail the audition, though.

When they reached the observatory they woke Eva and Honey. Having been awake for almost 48 hours, neither of them was very happy about this.

Despite the sound of birdsong and barking dogs, Eva refused to believe they had been returned to Earth. Even she was beginning to doubt her hold on reality. It didn't help that the data being sent in confirmed that the heavens had indeed shifted.

Honey rolled up her blanket and asked Albright for a lift back across the Atlantic, assuming it was still there.

CHAPTER 49

Salisbury thought twice about seeing Yuri. He knew it would be safer to wait until he had the opportunity to get reacquainted with the gin bottle, and called on Diana instead.

She was in the kitchen ironing while Julia still sat in front of television. He entered the back door and looked nervously about.

Knowing Diana had made the scholar think hard about the prejudices he had been brought up with. He usually thought twice about what he said to her yet, nevertheless, had to ask, 'Why are you ironing paper doilies?'

'Ran out of £10 notes. Tea?'

'Thank you.' Salisbury sat on a stool in the corner of the kitchen and tried to look inconspicuous.

'Have you seen Yuri?'

'Not yet.'

Diana nodded as though understanding why. There was an oddly domestic silence as the steam from her iron intimidated the floral pattern from yet another doily and transferred its imagine onto the ironing board. Salisbury picked up the book of government recommended recipes that lay open at his elbow. It was easy to tell how much panic had gone into collecting them. Any vegan could have compiled a volume far more efficiently in half the time. Now there was the singing of birds and barking of dogs, an uncomfortable pang struck him - the abattoirs would soon be back in business as well.

The kettle boiled and Diana distracted him from his misgivings.

'I hope Eva soon rings and tells me what's going on.'

'You don't believe we're back on Earth, then?'

For a few non-committal moments Diana furiously stirred the teabags then handed him a mug. 'It'd be too simple for those two. Why should they return us to the Earth?'

'Why not? All the animals appear to be here. The air smells a lot sweeter, so we must have our oceans back.'

'I don't know ...'

'You're just being suspicious for the sake of it.'

'As far as Dax and Reniola are concerned, it's a reflex action.'

Salisbury shrugged and took a sip of tea. 'I suppose I ought to try and get back home.'

'In that shirt?'

'Be chilly without it.'

'I may have one somewhere.' Diana went to the airing cupboard and pulled out a white shirt with a detachable collar.

Salisbury thanked her very much, promised to have it laundered as soon as he had finished with it, and knew better than to ask why she kept a man's shirt in the airing cupboard. By its immaculate condition, it couldn't have been Yuri's.

Before she returned to her ironing, Diana looked out of the window and saw Colonel Albright and Yuri in the meadow. 'Excuse me a moment, I want to see the Colonel before he leaves.'

'Certainly.' Salisbury didn't offer to join her; he knew what it was like to be a prune and didn't want to feel like a lemon as well.

As Diana strode out to meet him, Yuri fled back to his cottage, slamming its front door after him.

'What's the matter with Yuri?'

Albright smiled reassuringly. 'I think this whole business has got him down.

'Hardly surprising. Are you going now?'

'Very shortly. Things look as though they're back to normal.' '

The definition of "normal" has been somewhat altered.'

'Well... as normal as can be expected under the circumstances.'

Diana hesitated. Then the penny dropped. She folded her arms so the picture of Garfield on her T-shirt pulled a very peculiar face. 'And what circumstances would they be?'

The real Colonel wouldn't have tried to look so innocent in the face of an absurd question so it could only be one other entity.

'Well,' admitted Dax, 'there was a small complication Reniola didn't take into account when shifting the prehistoric Earth's largest moon.'

'When it comes to complications, Reniola deals in nothing small.'

'A mere historical detail.'

'What detail?'

'You're not going to be angry, are you?'

'Where's the point? It's never had any effect before.'

'Only, the reason why so many species, including

the dinosaurs, became extinct was because, about 60 million years ago, a comet was captured by the gravity of the Earth's largest moon and deviated towards the Earth. It took millions of years for the planet to recover, and most life forms were wiped out.'

'I see...' Diana didn't, but she wasn't going to give Dax the opportunity to evade.

'The comet knocked the larger moon out of its orbit. It fell towards the Sun and was vaporised. That's why Reniola didn't think there would be any harm in using it here as an alternative home for you humans.'

'Go on.'

'The problem she didn't compensate for was...'

'I'm listening.'

'Without this cataclysm, the dinosaurs would not have become extinct.'

'I should have known ...'

'Well... there was nothing we could do about it. They had first claim, you see. Once Moosevan had divided into smaller planet dwellers, they were happy to move to smaller worlds as long as they had no mobile life forms, just ecosystems and climates to organise. But the descendants of the dinosaurs...? We couldn't very well have evicted them, could we?'

'Having seen the table manners of their ancestors, it might have been a good idea.'

'And I'm sure it would help if you were all natural vegetarians, anyway.'

'But the animals have returned?'

'We'll have to do something about them as well.'

Before Diana could ask "as well as what?" They saw Salisbury pacing up the meadow towards them.

'If you ever do remember this conversation, you won't tell anyone else, will you?' Dax pleaded.

'Remember? I don't even know what planet we're on?'

'You're on the large moon that should have fallen

into the sun. Don't worry, though. There are plenty of oceans and the atmosphere is quite stable.'

'That's not the point is it,' growled Diana. 'How do you think the aggressive beggars on this planet will react if the Earth is filled with dinosaurs?'

'Oh, that won't be a problem.'

Salisbury was now close enough to catch the last comment. 'What won't be a problem?'

Dax gave a wry smile. 'Don't worry about it.'

The tone told Diana that there was every reason to worry. 'Why not?' she demanded.

'Because, history working out the way it did, you are now the descendants of dinosaurs who settled on this planet several million years ago to keep out of the way of the carnivores.'

'Don't be ridiculous! ' snapped Salisbury.

Dax gave a strangely innocent smile. The two humans reeled a little as their memories were scrambled, then nudged slightly to one side. They didn't notice Dax disappear, or even remember she had been there.

For a split second Diana thought Salisbury was a little taller than she recalled, and suddenly noticed those regimented waves in his whitish hair. Salisbury became aware of the ridges in Diana's skin, but was too much of a gentleman to stare. After all, they were only the legacy of the scales they had shed so many millions of years ago. Now they were true bipeds with spinal problems to match.

Diana swayed a little. 'I did come over strange then.'

'So did I,' agreed Salisbury. 'I wonder what caused it?'

'Must be something to do with the change in our diet. I'm not sure our systems are able to cope with so much gluten.'

'Well, you know what the dieticians say about us

eating cycads. Supposed to rot the brain.'

'You'd think we would have adapted by now.'

Salisbury rubbed his ear fin. 'Wouldn't surprise me if the home planet sent out agents to introduce some errant gene into the plantations. They could never forgive us for being herbivores. Now so many of them are becoming vegetarians, they should be taking advice from us.'

'Chance would be a fine thing. They really wanted us to become carnivores.'

'Who would we eat, for goodness sake?'

'As long as they don't start eating us again, who cares? I'd sooner have my brain rotted by cycads than eat what they do.'

'I have to admit that every now and then I'm curious to know what fish tastes like.'

'They smell so bad when out of water I'd have trouble getting near one.'

'They have to come ashore, though. It's the only way we can negotiate.'

'Home planet ate all the delegations sent to them.'

Salisbury felt uncomfortable and changed the subject. 'Look, I'll have to get back soon.'

'Papers to mark?'

'New curriculum.'

Diana realised. 'Oh, of course. You have to include monkey studies now, don't you?'

'Part of the new syllabus.'

'Revolting little creatures, always messing about with each others' private parts. Even fish are more civilised...' She sighed. 'Oh, I know... We have to treat our planet kindly and understand all its creatures. Monkeys, though! Home planet had the right idea there - they ate all of theirs as well.'

THE END

www.ingramcontent.com/pod-product-compliance
Lightning Source LLC
Chambersburg PA
CBHW050005070726
47592CB00018B/806